RECOMBINED

Book 3 in the Irrevocable Series

SAMANTHA JACOBEY

Lavish
Publishing LLC

First Edition

Book 3 of Irrevocable Series

All Rights Reserved

Published in the United States by Lavish Publishing, LLC, Midland, Texas

Cover Design by: OliviaProDesign

Cover Images: depositphotos.com

Paperback Edition

ISBN: 9780692440858

www.LavishPublishing.com

Contents

For my mother, Linda. Without her, much of this tale could not, or would not, have been written. Thank you for our family, which has taught me what crazy really means…

Prologue

"SHE'S PRECIOUS," the blonde whispered loudly, her face hovering above the tiny body in her arms. Her golden waves hung down next to her infant like a curtain, shielding her from the harsh overhead light.

Across the cramped space, Devon peered at his bride, the size of the hospital bed diminishing her large frame. "She is," he agreed. "You make beautiful babies, 'Manda." Standing, he shuffled closer, laying his giant left hand on her silky crown.

Shifting her eyes to gaze up at him, she sighed. "I'm really sorry I lied." She noted the dark circle that evidenced his punishment for her crime.

"Naw," he retorted easily. "Dey wouldn't o' been happy 'bout it then neither. Least now we don' have t' hide no more." Lifting his digits, he traced a tiny pudgy cheek. "I'm gonn' take good care o' you. Both o' you."

"I know you are." Amanda smiled weakly, hesitating a glance at the door. "But we can't stay here, Dev."

"Nope," he agreed crisply, leaning closer to rumble in a deep, gravelly voice. "Already workin' on dat." He stared at his ebony flesh, its contrast sharp against the milky white of his bride. "I'll get us home. Don' you worry. You jus' take care o' my little girl. Leave the schemin' t' me."

Amanda watched him, biting her lip and feeling the urge to cry. She had known all along their new angel had been his but had somehow convinced herself no one would know the difference. *How stupid of me.* She had a lot to make up for, to a lot of people, starting with the one sleeping against her chest.

Standing straight, he gathered his coat and gloves, preparing to leave. "I'll be back in a bit."

"Be careful," she called as his tall frame disappeared into the corridor.

Adjusting his knit cap, Devon made his way out the front door of the hospital, squinting into the bright light. Glancing at the jail house, where a large number of his comrades were being held, he exhaled loudly. For the moment, they were trapped, but not for long if things went his way. Spying the coffee shop across the narrow street, he made his way inside and ordered a cup of brew.

ONE

Many Hands

BAILEY EXHALED IN A SLOW HISS, her eyes scanning the massive cavern. "This place is amazing, Caleb." Moving forward, she timidly took in the smaller side rooms, finding a kitchen, med center, storage, and several living quarters. Across the great chamber, on the opposite side, she located another hallway. "Where does this go?"

"Two places, actually. Between here an' ground level," the blond supplied. "This's th' back storage, more densely packed for long term. We rotate the stock, so it holds th' freshest items, as far as food. Plus there's a smaller armory down here, more water, an' a place for personal items, kinda like a tiny general store."

The girl stared at him, her mind turning. "You have everything down here as well as up top?"

"'Xactly," Carson joined in, spouting what he knew. "It's th' back-up. If we ever had t' live down here, that'd be th' worst scenario, but we'd have everything in case somethin' happened t' all our stuff, houses an' cellars an' stuff."

"A massive bunker to hold out the world's greatest disasters." She nodded her understanding.

"Well, it was," Caleb corrected. "Now it's just a big hole in the ground."

When the girl gave him an odd look, he clarified, "It's the people that make this place special. Without 'em, it doesn't really mean anything." He wafted a hand towards the tunnel in question. "You can also reach th' surface this way through two other secret passages. We came in th' south entrance. You can also enter via th' greenhouse an' barn."

Thinking of the barn, his brow furrowed. "Man, we can't even rebuild. They took all our animals. Even if we get the people back, we got nothin' t' start with."

Together, the trio retraced their steps and exited the armory after shutting down the lights and securing the camouflage on their way out. Making the trek to the Cross house, Bailey had a small epiphany. "No wonder everyone got so bent out of shape about my post!"

"Yeah, pretty much," Caleb confirmed her theory. "No one outside o' the community knows about Lawson. No eyes have ever seen it. No other hands helped t' build it. It's entirely ours, an' we can't run it without everyone. The dream of a handful o' people an' the home we hoped we would never need t' live in."

Bailey sighed, aware of their unhappiness, as well as her own. "What do you suppose they did with them? I mean, why take the people?"

"Well, they took all th' munitions an' the food. They couldn't leave the people here t' starve," he theorized while they climbed onto the porch. "Hopefully they're being treated ok an' weren't taken to another location simply t' be eliminated."

Carson's expression shifted to shock. "They wouldn' do that!"

"They might've. O' course if they were gonna do that, I think they woulda killed 'em here an' left 'em, same as the others." His older brother grimaced. "You said you buried some of our *menfolk*." He clamped the smaller male on the shoulder. "Where, an' who were they?"

"I used the li'l backhoe an' dug a hole behind the armory. It was Jim, Bill, an' Allen." He looked grave, giving them a shrug. "I didn' know what else t' do."

"I'm sure it was better than leaving them wherever they lay." Bailey's lip quivered. "Jim was a really nice old man, too."

Caleb glared at her for a moment, unsure if he should enlighten her about the men who had been permanently removed from the group. Deciding against it, he caught a wisp of her auburn waves, pushing it back away from her face. "There's really nothin' we can do about them. What we can do is form a plan. It took many hands t' build this place, an' we owe it to our friends an' family to at least try t' get them back."

"I totally agree." The girl stood straighter. "So what should we do first? Even if we are able to locate them and break them out somehow, we can't defend ourselves. The front gate is standing wide open."

"We need t' block it up somehow," Carson suggested, slamming his right fist into his left palm. "Then when they come after us, we stand on the wall an' shoot 'em."

"Except they have a helicopter, so that wouldn't really work. They could shoot us instead or land inside the walls again, an' there wouldn't be much we could do t' stop them," Caleb used a low tone, not wanting to stop the flow of ideas even as he pointed out the obvious flaws. "Besides, if we block up the entrance, we have t' go all th' way around t' the stable gate t' get in."

"So move the gate and block up that entrance," Bailey suggested with a faint grin.

Caleb stared off into the distance, as if he could see the access in question through the buildings that obstructed his view. "Even if it would fit," he finally admitted, "we couldn't do it with only th' three of us. Havin' the equipment would help, but we would still need a little more muscle to accomplish it."

"So what can we do?" Carson had begun to feel a little hopeless.

"We clean up th' mess for one," Caleb assumed command easily, "an' hope that th' weather breaks. We still need t' get a better idea o' what all they removed, or should I say what they left us. What the bastards took don' matter much at this point. In the end, I'm sure they'll come back for more when the snow clears, so we definitely need t' be ready for that."

Bailey stared at him with a bleak expression, finding his evaluation a bit discomforting. Timidly, she laced her fingers with his for a moment, taking comfort in his strength. "Which building should we start with?"

"Le's start with this 'ne." He indicated the house attached to their current location. "Clean out the bedrooms, put everything back into the closets, an' make it livable again. You can take Mom an' Dad's room." He noticed her slight pout at the suggestion. "Unless you still wanna group up in the livin' room."

Staring down the road at the wide-open entrance she could see in the distance, she nodded. "At least until the walls are back up, I'd rather be closer at hand."

"All right. Clean up, like I said, but we can still sleep in th' front room together like we have been," he agreed, giving her hand a squeeze before releasing her. "You go in an' get started on that, an' I'm gonna make sure there's nothin' goin' on in any o' the buildings that needs immediate attention, any leaks or anything."

Bailey gave him a small nod. "I guess Carson's going with you?"

"Sure," he agreed. "An' we'll be back at twelve if you wanna have a little lunch ready for us."

"That I can do." She smiled at the comfort the familiar routine gave her. Watching them walk away, in the direction of the med center, her heart began to pound heavily in her chest. Giving the snow-covered pavement another long stare, she heaved a deep sigh, then made her way inside to begin her task.

Starting at the highest and furthest point in the house, she gathered the items that had been strewn about in the master bedroom. Clothes and personal items she stuffed into trash bags for the mistress of the property to sort through when she returned. Tossing the sheets over the banister, she clomped down the steps to put them into the washer so the beds would be ready for whoever needed them when the time came.

Working her way through the other bedrooms, she discovered that it was Caleb's mattress that had been provided for her, so she threw all of his ransacked items into the hall to wash for him and finished the room itself from there. Moving on to Carson's, she had a better idea of what she wanted to accomplish, so it went fairly quickly.

Tackling the upstairs bathroom, she knocked it out, then hauled the boys' laundry down, making sure to remake the beds as she had intended with the clean sheets. By the time lunch came around, she had all but completed the cozy dwelling and set about preparing a hot meal for her cohorts, fairly certain they would need one.

When the hands on the clock read noon, Bailey began to grow concerned, pacing the small kitchen and checking on her makeshift meal. With nothing to directly occupy her, she began to contemplate their situation and the events of the last few days and weeks. Quickly realizing worrying over her brothers was a lost cause, she purposely steered clear of that topic and considered what might be taking place back in Midland instead.

Recalling their last trip to Wal-Mart, probably the most popular store in town, it had been quite a shock to see so many of the shelves emptied completely. *Of course, there had been a shortage even before news of the snowstorm had spread.* Having the bad weather had only added fuel to the fire. Staring into space for a moment, she wondered if Mark really had stayed at his post until the last burger had been served, shaking her head at the very idea of such a thing.

Leaving her pots on over a low flame to stay warm, Bailey took a peek outside, walking from one end of the porch to the other. To her dismay, the snow fell in sheets, obviously heavier than it had been before, and appeared to be in no way letting up. Peering into the thick haze, she could make out the diner and picked up on the faint sound of voices from that direction the best she could tell.

Assuming they belonged to her men, she decided to give them another half hour before she became panicked enough to go investigate. Returning to the warmth inside, she stood in the doorway and glared at the living area they had shared the night before. *This room doesn't need much right now since we're still using it.*

The room itself good-sized, it covered about one third of the first floor, with the kitchen beyond taking up another third. Immediately to the left of the entrance lay a small cubicle, which was the only remaining room to be put back in order. To the right of that lay the stairs, and between those and the kitchen lay a narrow hallway, which led to another bathroom on the left underneath them and the laundry room on the right.

With a small sigh, she tackled the last room in the house, which was a complete shambles. The small area had been set aside as an office, with a desk and a computer, and nothing, including the desk, was where it should have been.

All of their paperwork had been overturned and tossed about and the drawers all dumped into a pile. *Whatever they had been looking for, I'm certain they found.* Setting up the tower and monitor, Bailey reconnected all of the lines, her mind turning in the process. *The sheriff jumped the gun coming here before Martial Law had been instituted, if it has been yet at all.*

Of course, she realized that could have been the point. The residents were obviously prepared to defend themselves, violently if necessary, but had not anticipated the attack at such an early point in the chain of events. *I wonder how long those guys had been planning this.*

Watching the screen flicker to life, she considered how much Caleb knew about this rogue group of officers, as he had not seemed surprised they had been the aggressors in the end. Seeing that the internet connection remained, she smiled faintly. *Well, the rest of the world hasn't completely disappeared yet.*

Pulling up a browser, she navigated to yahoo, where she discovered that the media machine still rolled, at least for the time being. The horrific pictures gave her a deep ache in the pit of her stomach, and a moment later, tears began to trickle down her cheeks at the blatant way the images of men, women, and children caught for eternity in their moment of suffering were brazenly displayed at the top of each story.

Dear God, she breathed, *Caleb was right!* The plague had not been enough in itself but complicated the issue with the earthquakes and ice storms. *Oh, and don't forget the cluster of hurricanes that bombarded the east coast right at the end of the season. Those poor people in Florida—flooded and then frozen within a matter of a month.* Even the outbreak of volcanic eruptions from the summer before could have been a contributing factor, as it had set the stage.

She recalled how each and every disaster had been followed by a cascade of media hype, adding to the social unrest. *It's not right, the way the ratings machine worked—nothing of value and all sensationalized.* Wiping at her trails of sadness, she closed the connection, thankful they had escaped. *The frog is definitely boiling,* she sighed.

TWO

On Our Own

HEARING the sound of her comrades entering through the kitchen, Bailey shifted quickly into the small downstairs lavatory and washed her face. Joining them when she had restored her features the best she could, she discovered they had served themselves and were sitting at the table, devouring the dishes.

"I was beginning to worry," she teased, filling a bowl of her own.

"Well"—Caleb grinned—"once we got started, it was kinda hard t' stop." Noticing the red that stood out around her eyes, he watched her take her seat. Casting a quick glance at the boy next to him, he asked more quietly, "Everything ok here?"

"Yes." She avoided looking at him. "Everything is in order, in fact." She stirred her stew for a moment. "I got the computer hooked up, and we still have access to the outside world." She lifted her gaze to meet his, not wanting to verbally share what she had seen in too much detail. "It's not good."

"Damn." He broke the connection, continuing to eat for a short time before saying anything else. "At least we aren't there, seein' it firsthand," he muttered a few minutes later. He knew their small taste at Wal-Mart on the way out of town had been quite enough.

"Right!" she echoed his sentiment. "But we definitely need to get the grounds secured, which means we have to get the gate repaired one way or the other."

"Yeah." He nodded. "I've been thinkin' about that, an' I took a few measurements. The gates are actually th' same size, so we could make the switch an' block up the cattle entrance. Plus, we have the horse arena. We can dismantle that for the beams t' do it with. We'd pretty much have to since it's such a large expanse an' it needs t' be sturdy."

"That's good thinking," she replied. "But how are you going to do that in the middle of a snowstorm?"

"Very carefully."

Frowning heavily, she wondered if he was pulling her leg. "Well, I guess I could help."

"No." He cut her off before she could go any further. "You need to take care o' restorin' order t' all o' the buildings. Take inventory o' what we have left that we can use." Leaning back in his chair, he pushed his empty dish away. "You said the internet still works?"

"Yes. I was looking at the news when you came in."

"Good. We're gonna head back over t' the diner an' finish boardin' that up. Plus get th' rest o' the windows in the houses before nightfall. You jump back on there an' message everyone in the group or make a post. I don't care, but somehow we need t' let 'em know we're here."

"You think they will see it?" she gasped.

"I have no idea." He ran his fingers around the outside of his lips. "It's just in case, really. If for some reason one o' them was t' get access, they would know."

"All right," she agreed reluctantly. "I'll message them individually. How are you boarding everything up? Are you tearing out the walls and moving them?"

"No." He chuckled, realizing that she hadn't seen all of what lay hidden at The Ranch by a long shot. "Not all o' the garages have cars in them. In fact, only a few o' them hold vehicles. One o' them is stacked with sheets o' plywood an' other buildin' materials. We have some glass but not nearly enough t' repair all o' th' windows they busted, so coverin' 'em will have t' do."

"Jesus, you guys really did think of everything!" she praised in awe.

Caleb only grinned, standing to help himself to more coffee. "We got a lotta work ahead of us, little bit. I'm not gonna sugarcoat it. This's supposed t' be the last day o' the snow, right?"

"Actually, I don't recall seeing any new predictions." She rose to begin the cleanup. "All they are reporting at the moment is the mayhem. But on the way down, that was the last forecast—three days of snow. So I think it will be today or tomorrow."

"All right," he agreed. "So we keep workin' on the interiors an' shorin' up the buildings an' hope that tomorrow we catch a break. I figure we have a week at best, after it stops, before they come back for whatever else they wanna get. Provided they don' decide t' move their own people in here."

"Why would they move their own people in here?" Her eyes narrowed.

"This place was designed t' provide resources, t' feed the group an' all that. You gotta admit it's pretty sweet. I'm sure they'll at some point decide t' colonize it an' make use of our facilities," he offered his assessment while slipping on his jacket. "Don' worry about that right now. After you're done here, I suggest you tackle th' ranch house. When we get our people back, it'll make more sense t' crowd into th' larger building t' conserve what we can, at least at th' beginning."

"Ok," she agreed with a slight nod. "So we're pretty safe as long as the snows falling, you think?"

"Yeah," he agreed, reaching for her and catching the back of her head with his right hand. Allowing his thumb to trace the line of her ear, his clear blue eyes bore into her. "We gotta be tough, Bailey. Things are likely t' get worse before they get better."

Stepping towards him, she flung her arms around his broad

shoulders, ignoring the damp feel of his jacket pressed against her. "I know," she managed, squeezing him as tightly as she could.

His arms found their way around her waist, hugging her snugly against him. "Get your chores done, Bailey-girl, an' dress warm when you go outside." He nuzzled the top of her head. "We'll see you after dark." Turning to go, he had one more command. "Oh, an' I need you t' cover th' windows."

"Excuse me?"

"Take some blankets an' hang 'em over th' windows t' help insulate 'em," he offered the reason, hoping she would accept it.

"Ok." She grinned, not questioning his motives.

With a brief wave, Caleb collected his brother, and the pair made their way through the wind-driven snow. Arriving at the diner, they finished hanging the plywood over the last few openings and gathered their tools.

"She don' know much," Carson commented quietly.

"No," his older brother agreed. "But she's learnin'," he voiced his approval of the girl.

"It's not safe," he continued to push. "She could get us killed."

"She's fine." Caleb stopped moving and faced him squarely. "We're on our own, Cars, an' we need each other. We all have our place, an' I don' wanna hear nothin' else about it."

His blue eyes blinking slowly beneath his bright red hair, Carson adjusted his cap anxiously. "Why'd you pick her?" he demanded, his displeasure at his brother's choice obvious.

An uncomfortable silence followed as Caleb dropped his glare and finished preparing to get on to the next structure. Leading the younger Cross to the Burns-Tate duplex, he felt his gut twist at the accusation. Inside, he began to measure the few windows that had been shattered. "I didn' pick her," he admitted quietly.

Jotting down the numbers, they moved to the garage behind the structure to select their wood and make the necessary cuts.

"I know you don' get it yet," he spoke sternly while looking over his choices, "but someday you will."

"Ok." The boy pouted slightly. "So why her? What makes her so special?"

"She's jus' the one, Carson." He stopped moving, cutting his eyes over to glare at him. "She's exactly that—special. She's stronger than you or anyone else aroun' here realizes. Smart, caring, loyal." He paused, glancing around nervously. "Don' say anything t' her about this."

"'Bout what?" He wrinkled his nose.

"About her an' me an' stuff like that. Jus' let it be. We ain' talked about it, an' now ain't the time," the blond insisted. "Maybe when we get settled an' some idea o' what the future holds, but not now." Giving his brother an icy stare, he commanded more loudly, "You got me?" In a flash, he punched his younger sibling in the shoulder for emphasis.

"Yeah, I got you!" Carson shot back, massaging the appendage through the thick jacket.

"Ok, le's get this done." Caleb returned to work. "We only got so much daylight, an' then we need to be back inside."

"Tha's why you had 'er cover the window, huh? So no one sees th' lights."

"Yeah." He exhaled loudly. "I don' know that anybody would, but jus' in case."

Throwing themselves into the process, the pair completed that dwelling and the one across the street. Noting the dark outside had begun settling into actual night, they packed their gear and trudged back to the house, where only a soft glow could be seen as they got closer.

"It's not completely dark," Carson commented.

"No, but it's not bright," Caleb pointed out. "An' it'll have t' do. Leave it alone," he instructed, stomping the snow off his boots on the back step.

Inside, the smell of another vegetable and noodle stew greeted them, and he chuckled at the sight of the cornbread. "I think we'll have to make another trip into Lawson, maybe tomorrow. We got some meat down there."

"Canned?" she inquired, recalling the hog they had preserved over the summer.

"Yup, plus whatever's in that giant freezer," he agreed with a grin. "Don' get me wrong. I love how you're makin' the best o' what we got. But we're gonna need a little more sustenance, especially with the cold."

"True." She returned his smile. "We can do that." Taking her seat, she pushed on, "Would you like to hear my report?"

"Sure." He played along, glad to see she seemed in better spirits.

"Well, everything here is in order, and I put all of you guys' clothes away." She grinned at the younger of the two, hoping he would be pleased with her efforts. "I also tackled the ranch house and bagged up everyone's stuff over there. What do you think those guys were looking for?"

"Whadda you mean?" Caleb crumbled more of the bread into his bowl.

"They ransacked everything, but it didn't look as if anything was missing, except the food. And the people, of course." She flicked her eyes between them. "They didn't even take the computers."

"I'm sure they took what appeared t' be o' value," he supplied, "an' money'll be pretty worthless. Weapons, ammunition, an' food'll be high on th' list. An' they took the big radio outta the diner, so I bet all the handhelds are gone, too. They might've come in handy at some point, but again, we can't worry about that."

"I didn't find any radios, so I suppose you're right. You know who they are, don't you," her voice grew quiet, "and where they've taken everyone."

"I have an idea." He nodded, dropping his tone as well. "One thing at a time, little bit. Tomorrow, we finish with the buildings an' gettin' our inventory. After that, we see what we can do about the gate. I think we may seal up the front. Even if we have t' go around the side t' get in an' out with vehicles. That means anyone tryin' t' get in will have to as well, an' that could work to our advantage."

The girl swallowed, her eyes growing wide. "Do you really think they'll come back here?"

"Yeah." He dusted his hands noisily. "I tol' you I'm not gonna sugarcoat it. We need t' get set. How'd the messaging go?" he changed the subject easily.

"It went fine. I copied and pasted the same to all. *The Ranch is secured, and we are preparing for your return. Please advise your situation and what we can do to help.* That's it. I didn't want to get too specific in case someone else were to gain access to the information." She toyed with her spoon, trying to evaluate his expression.

"That's good," he praised. Eating for a few minutes, he finished the meal before he shared what he knew. Rising to clear away his empties, he supplied, "There's a township about eight miles south o' th' main turn-off, founded about five years ago. It was a real problem when they moved in. Made th' *menfolk* pretty nervous."

"And why is that?" she queried, joining him in the cleanup.

Not taking his eyes off his work, he exhaled loudly. "That's a bit of a long story. Le's get everything taken care of, an' I'll tell you about it once we're settled for bed." He cut his gaze over, smiling at the girl genuinely and grateful that she had opted to share the living area for the time being. *This way we get to be close, an' Carson can be our chaperone.*

THREE

Too Close for Comfort

BAILEY RELUCTANTLY ALLOWED the process to continue until they had put the kitchen in order and everyone had washed up and dressed for bed. Stretching out on her mattress, she slid beneath the covers, noting that Caleb resumed his position on the sofa, although he could not see down the road with the thick covering over the front glass.

Apparently making the same observation, the man allowed her to settle in, then doused the lights and tied the blanket back so he would in fact have a view of the road in front of the house. Or at least he would have once the snow quit falling.

"You think it's going to stop soon?" she alluded to the swirling flakes.

"I have no idea." He stared at the white blanket through narrow slits after he finished securing the cloth. "I have to admit it kinda concerns me. We never got snow, or rarely did, I should say. This's odd, gettin' so much of it. An' I'm on th' fence with how I feel about it. It does make things harder for us, but at th' same time, it makes it harder for them, too."

Turning to his place of rest, he covered himself in a half-reclined position, taking in her prone form in the near darkness.

"It's called Pouty, the town is. I think it's named after the guy who put it together. They built everything from scratch—planned it all, kinda like we did, only at a much larger scale. They got a charter an' all the governmental paperwork, so they're legal. The county sheriff had a hand in it, but they got an actual police department there, too."

"Really." She stared at the blond spikes glistening in the shadow. "So it's a big place?"

"Not really," he elaborated. "A few hundred people. Devon an' Luis came here about a year before those guys set up. They went an' did some recon after it became clear they was here t' stay. Nung had been here since I was a kid, an' he didn't like it at all. Too close for comfort, he said. But he's not part o' the *menfolk*, so I don' think they really listened t' what he had t' say."

"Looks like maybe they should have," she countered quietly.

"Yeah." He shifted uncomfortably, cutting his eyes over at his brother, who observed from his smaller set of cushions in silence. "You prolly figured out our community don't take kindly t' strangers. Or newcomers, for that matter." He glared at the window again, becoming lost in the past for a moment, allowing it to swallow him. "Nung didn't like it, an' Don wasn't here yet. So, Devon an' Luis made a few trips over to poke around. There may be more o' them, but they're jus' as guarded as we are."

"They put up buildings, arranged so that there's a jail an' center o' town with the houses surroundin' it. Plus, they put in a few apartment buildings or condos, so they are packed in there pretty good. No wall, though. I went over a few times on my bike an' had a look. Ate at the diner an' flirted with a few o' the local girls a couple o' years ago." He grinned at his few attempts at interacting with women outside of his small hometown. "Some o' their guys made it clear pretty quick that I wasn't welcome there an' their women were off limits."

"Did they know you were from here?" Her eyes grew wide in the darkness.

"I don't think so." He shrugged. "It was the principal o' the thing." He paused for a few moments, his mind sifting over the time after that. "We left them alone for th' most part, an' they didn't seem too interested in us. So it was quite a surprise that they would attack us like they did."

"Maybe they weren't ready and needed the stores of food," she suggested, growing tired after her long day of chores. "Or they might have needed the animals, either to eat or for breeding."

"Yeah, I'm sure that was part o' their motivation. But the food won't last that many people long." He shifted his gaze to watch her, hearing her voice fade. "I think tomorrow we should be able to finish the houses. Then we can start on the pens."

"The pens?" Carson piped up, having finally heard something that pertained to him. "Why would we bother with that? They got all our animals, so they prolly slaughtered 'em, don' ya think?"

"No, I don't believe so," Bailey quietly agreed with the older male. "They took them to use as stock, the same as we were. We'll get their homes ready the same as ours, and if we get the chance, we'll steal them back as well as our people."

Caleb smiled at her wording, placing herself in the *we* of the group. "Goodnight, Bailey," he called softly across the small space.

"Goodnight, Caleb," she retorted before she lost consciousness.

Leaving the hospital, Devon crossed the street and entered the diner for his evening meal and a cup of coffee. Sliding into a booth facing the entrance to the medical facility, he didn't bother to look up when Don took the seat opposite him.

"Hidy," the younger man proffered. "How's your wife?" He snickered slightly, having had his fill of the girl and passed her on.

"She's doin' ok. They's still keepin' an eye on 'er. Say she's anemic." Glancing up, he recognized Phillip Pipes and offered him a hand. "Hey, Phil. Wha's up?"

Shaking the dark appendage vigorously, their new friend sank down onto the cushion next to Don. "Can you guys believe this snow? We've been here a few years and haven't ever seen so much as a flake. Then we get this blizzard." He laughed anxiously. "Makes me wonder if we shoulda taken a place further south."

"I knows," Devon agreed. "Good thing you guys showed up an' we got the stores cleared out 'fore it hit. Who knows how long it woulda been if we hadn't."

"I know that's right." The other man ran his hand over his balding scalp while he ordered a cup for himself. "You likin' your place, Don?"

"Oh, yeah," the man next to him agreed. "It's not real big, but since I ain't got a woman, it suits me fine."

"Well, don't you worry none. Plenty o' women here. I'm sure it won't take you long to settle down." Phil smiled, flicking his wedding band and shifting the conversation to the other man. "So, when's your wife gonna be ready to go home? We got your place lined out…whenever you wanna see it, o' course. That last set of condos we built are for housing our new families as they form, so one o' them goes to you."

"I'm thinkin' dey let her out tomorra," Devon provided, considering his bride and their child briefly. "When will we be gettin' back to Da Ranch?" He sipped from his cup, maintaining his calm poker face. "If'n dats still da plan."

"Not until the snow clears a bit, at the soonest. Maybe not 'til spring. Settle in here, guys. We got nothin' but time. That place is deserted an' not goin' anywhere." Grinning at his most highly regarded recruits, Phil stood, taking in the rest of the nearly empty diner. "I'll see you later," he dropped casually, on his way out the door.

As soon as he had gone, Luis slid into the vacated spot, adopting a much lower tone. "We can't wait too long." He had been listening from the counter while flirting with the waitress, pretending to mind his own business. "You know eventually some-one's gonna get a meal outta th' Knight stores, and then things are gonna get ugly."

"Yeah," Don agreed with a nod. "I been thinking the same thing. When we stacked everything, we put it in the back, so maybe it'll take a few weeks to get that far down, an' we'll be gone by then."

His dark eyes flicking around at the other patrons, Devon nodded slightly. "Play it cool, fellas. Certain people are gettin' things ready for us over there. If they make us wait more 'an a week, we may make a break for it."

"That's an awful risk. All the other men an' half the women are locked up in that stockade o' theirs." Don frowned heavily.

"So figure out how you're gonna get 'em out." Devon's features remained placid. "You"—he pointed at Luis—"get a line on our young 'uns. An' I'll take care o' their equipment. We'll need some transportation, an' whatever we don' take'll need t' be eliminated."

Don grinned, pleased with the idea of hurting the group after seeing his friends shot five days before. Leaning back in his cushion seat, he gazed at the man across from him. "We can do that." Flagging the waitress, he felt ready to have a bit of dinner followed by a good night's sleep.

FOUR

Snow Angel

BAILEY AWOKE the following morning to a soft glow filtering in from the drawn blanket. Blinking at the window frame, she could make out the shadow of Caleb, dark against the light, coffee mug in hand. Sliding quietly out of her nest, she sidled up next to him to enjoy the view.

Noticing the auburn hair, Caleb placed his hand tentatively on the small of her back. "Good mornin', little bit."

"Good morning," she replied, pushing her way in front of him slightly and folding her arms across the wood-framed lower pane to lean on. "God, this reminds me of home." The swirl of flakes had come to an end, and a white blanket covered everything seen from their vantage point.

Resting his cup on the bookcase to his right, Caleb freed his other hand. Boldly pushing it around her belly to embrace her from behind, his left fingers found their way to her head and tenderly weaved through the hairs to massage her scalp. "I think I see the beauty after all," he breathed against her right ear, giving her chills at the intimate act.

"I told you it was there." She grinned, her mind leaping to Ked for a moment with his bold and grasping manner. Allowing her best friend to hold her, she whispered, "It's almost a shame to disturb it."

"I know. Like I said, we've only had snow here a few times, an' I'm not even sure Carson was old enough t' remember it." He glanced over at the slumbering boy, not wishing him to see the display the couple would make against the growing daylight.

Shifting her gaze so that she could see the younger male as well, she mused aloud, "Maybe we should enjoy it a bit today. Play in it a little, while we can."

"Maybe so." He tightened his grip on her, feeding on her willingness to be held. Pushing his nose against her, he blew warm air across her ear. "I think you may be my snow angel, Bailey," his voice low, his words were only for her.

She gasped with a wide grin, her breath creating a small amount of fog on the glass. "I thought we were just friends." She used a finger to make dots in the coating.

Nuzzling her, he felt reluctant to let her go. "We are," he quipped, a little more loudly. "I was testing you." Dropping his hands, he turned away, grabbing the empty mug to refill with steaming brew. "You want some o' this coffee?"

"I don't drink coffee." She remained for a moment, saddened by the removal of his warm embrace. "Did I pass?"

Caleb only laughed, digging through their supplies for what looked like breakfast. "I guess it's an acquired taste," he referred to the beverage. "You can play with him for a bit. I bet he'd like that."

Joining him after a trip to the bathroom to shower and dress, the girl began to prepare the meal, while Caleb roused the boy, sending him to do the same. Watching him stretch on his way up the stairs, Bailey smiled briefly before her thoughts grew dark. "You think Jess and Jase are ok?"

"Sure they're ok. Why wouldn't they be?" He took a seat on a kitchen chair to watch her.

"They were taken, remember? Along with everyone else. I wonder if anyone got my message yesterday," she pondered aloud.

"Well, I can check. What's your login?" Jotting down her details on a scrap of paper, Caleb left her to her chore. Firing up the computer, he sighed with pleasure to see the internet connection. *Well, we're not totally gone.* Opening the browser and navigating to Facebook, he entered her information and whooped at the sight of the little red one. "Someone did!" he called to her in the other room.

Clicking the inbox, he discovered it had been Devon, late last night. His reply seemed cryptic: *See you soon.* Blinking at the screen for a moment, he noticed the girl planting herself beside him. "Whadda you make o' that?"

"I have no idea." She sounded breathless, her mind racing. "Is it the only one?"

"Yeah." He checked the news feed, then logged off to try his own account. Finding nothing, he directed her back to the morning meal. "You guys go ahead an' have a bit o' fun, but not too long. If he's plannin' on seein' us soon, we need t' be as ready as we can be."

"Yes," she agreed, putting plates on the table.

Carson joined them with his damp red hair sticking out in chunks. "We're gonna play in the snow?" he inquired while sliding into his chair.

"Sure." His brother grinned. "You like snow?"

"Not really." He made a face. "It makes a terrible mess outta everything, so it's not really all that great to me." He glared at the girl with distrust.

Bailey laughed out loud, Caleb smiling at her lightened mood. "I'll show you how to build a snowman," she cajoled. "And make you some hot chocolate, although I'm not sure how it's going to taste with the powdered milk."

"Mix it up now," the blond offered. "Put it in the fridge while you play. I think it tastes better after it's aged a bit."

"Huh." She shook her head. "I'll try it. I wasn't real impressed with the batch I made yesterday."

As soon as she had finished her meal, Bailey prepared the

white liquid and placed the container in the refrigerator, frowning slightly at the device as the door closed. *At least we still have a few comforts, for as long as the turbines last anyways.* "Do they have electricity over in Pouty?"

"Oh yeah." Caleb nodded. "They got some big windmills for that an' water, same as us. If they had copied our wall, I woulda said we were their inspiration." He chuckled loudly.

"Hmmp," she grunted. "They shoulda left us alone," she mumbled under her breath.

Picking up the hiking boots she had retrieved from the ranch house, the girl laced them up and shoved her foot inside, pleased that they still fit. "Well, I think these will be better. I hate when my feet get wet." She wafted a hand at her sneakers that were still drying by the back door. Turning to the boys she indicated the outside. "Let's get moving, shall we?"

Carson's crinkled features appeared hesitant, but he followed the girl, donning his coat, gloves, and a knit cap beneath the hood of his jacket. A few minutes later, they were working together, pushing a massive, albeit lopsided, ball of snow. Helping her form the second segment, his mood improved, and he began to laugh and speak more openly.

"Your brothers did this back home?" His flushed lips curled. "I don' really like the cold," he admitted slightly under his breath.

"Yes. Every year." Her breath frosted heavily in her excitement. "Jess and Jase both love the snow. I'm sure wherever they are, they're driving everyone nuts, wanting to get out in it." She briefly pictured her younger siblings and their yard back in Illinois.

Sensing her diminished mood, Carson reassured her while patting snow to fill in the low spots. "I'm sure they're ok. You'd be pretty sick t' hurt a kid, an' I don' think they would."

"I have to agree," she nodded. "It's funny though. I never really cared if they were around back then. Now…" She paused, reflecting on her past. "Now, I can't imagine my life without them."

At that moment, Caleb joined them, lifting the smallest sphere to place it atop the stack. "Not bad," he praised. Slapping his younger sibling on the back, he continued, "You ready t' get some work done?"

"Yes, sir." He brushed the red hairs that stuck out from his cap with a salute.

"Good. Bailey can continue with gettin' the houses in order, an' you an' I'll go make sure the pens are ready. We need t' double-check the horse stalls as well."

"Yes, sir." The girl waved, smiling to herself as she plodded up the path towards the towering structure in the farthest corner of the estate.

FIVE

God's Creatures

BAILEY GRINNED BROADLY as she crunched through the thick white blanket of frost in her new boots. *Boy that was fun,* she reflected on her adventure with the youngest Cross. *It's hard to imagine having never played in the snow before.* Her thoughts shifting to her younger brothers, her smile lessened. *I wish they could have been here.*

Climbing the steps to the veranda, she reminded herself that they would be back, and their family would be whole again. *What's left of it will be, anyways.* Making her way into the kitchen, she forced the dark thoughts from her mind, throwing herself fully into the task at hand.

She had worked her way through the house, for the most part, the day before, but wanted to finish up with each of the beds and common areas. Recalling her time as part of the household the summer before, she took special care with the bathrooms before she put the large living area in order and tackled the kitchen.

Running a sink full of warm suds, she washed the few items that had been left in the kitchen, her mind still turning what would be next on her list. When she had finished, she swept and mopped the floor, then gave the room a satisfied sigh from the doorway. *I bet even Connie would be pleased.*

Closing the exit behind her, she decided to cross the small section of ground and tackle the Knight residence next since the guys had already repaired the only busted glass—the large picture window that spanned the front, measuring six feet across. "That's a real shame," she muttered, peeking into the living area through one of the narrower panes that flanked the new plywood.

As she did so, the girl froze, picking up on an odd sound. Her hand suspended for a moment, she slowly rested it against the painted trim, focused on listening to the silence. Again, she heard it —a distinctive squealing that brought Carson's story of eating a rat to the front of her mind.

"Surely not," she spoke aloud, turning to notice snow had begun to drift lightly to the ground again. *Damn.*

Moving to the door, she shuddered at the idea of being confronted by vermin when she entered the structure. Pushing against the large wooden portal, she heard the sound again, louder this time, and she realized it emanated from directly beneath her. Curiosity getting the better of her, she closed the entrance and trotted down the stairs to investigate.

The porch itself stood about three feet off the ground, as did the house. Under it, a covering made of wooden lattice allowed her to see beneath. Scraping a section of snow out of the way so that her knees could make contact with actual earth, she grimaced into the darkened space.

Not seeing anything but black, she pressed her face against the slats, allowing her eyes to slowly adjust to the lack of light. A few minutes later, she realized she was seeing a pair of eyes staring back at her. Drawing a deep breath, she focused on remaining calm, aware that some type of animal had become trapped beneath the structure.

Watching the yellow spheres blink a few times as they bore into her, a wave of panic twisted her gut. "Oh my God. Are you a coyote?" The realization that the front gate had been down for days and there was no telling what had wandered in caused her voice to tremble. However, as soon as her words were out, she could see a large, bushy tail begin to wag. *Holy shit. It's a dog!*

Leaning back, she sank her fingers through the diamond-shaped holes, grasping the underpinning as an anchor while she surveyed the length of the porch from where she knelt. "I don't see any holes, baby. How'd you get in there?"

Rising, a little stiff from the cold and the awkward position, she kicked the snow away from the edge of the porch all the way down until she reached the corner, thankful her new footwear made the task easier. *And more comfortable.* Turning, she continued the six feet or so, until she reached the place where the house met the mesh; there, she located a fairly decent sized hole. Only hesitating for a moment, she poked her head inside and called to the creature that had curled up below the front door.

Lifting its head to look at her, the animal didn't move. However, as soon as it did, a few loud squeals echoed under the cramped space, and the girl recognized the noise. "You've got puppies!" she called loudly, a surge of excitement washing over her. Pulling her head back out into the swirling flakes, she knew she needed to move quickly.

Looking around wildly, she had no idea where the boys would be. Shading her eyes against the biting wind that appeared to be gaining strength, she glared down the road that led to the other side of the compound where the stables and barn lay. *Of course!*

Taking off in a run, Bailey made it to the far end in a matter of minutes. Panting heavily when she pushed through the double doors at the end closest to the rabbit cages, she halted in her tracks. Before her, the two young men were doing their best to clean up the area where she had disposed of her assailant two days prior.

"Caleb!" she practically screamed, causing him to stand straight up, an expression of panic flittering across his rugged features.

Giving her a quick inspection, he didn't see any obvious injuries and demanded bluntly, "What's up? Is someone here?"

"Not that I know of." She grinned with anxious excitement. "I found something you have to see. But we have to hurry. It started snowing again, and I have no idea how long she's got before she freezes to death."

"She who?" Carson butted into the conversation, dropping his shovel and preparing to follow the girl who had exited the swinging door in a flash. Marching down the road at a quick pace, he pumped his arms vigorously. "Who'd you find, Bailey?" His voice had picked up an agitated tone when she failed to answer the first time.

"Not who," the girl corrected, reaching to clasp Caleb's hand and give it a squeeze. "I found a dog!"

"A dog?!?" The latter used the connection to yank her to a stop. "What kind of dog? And where?"

"I don't know what kind." She smiled. "I can't see that well. It's hiding under the Knight porch, and it has puppies!"

"Bailey, there's no dogs here!" his voice became panicked.

"Yeah, there is." The younger male adjusted his cap against the rising wind. "It showed up outside th' gate a few weeks ago, an' Don Finch let it in. Said it was bad luck t' harm one o' God's creatures without just cause."

"Really?" Caleb considered his words for a moment. "Was it pregnant?"

"Don' really know," his brother supplied with a shrug. "I only saw her once, an' she didn' look like it then. But that was a few weeks ago, like I said, when she got here. After a couple o' days, an' the new wore off, I think everyone kinda forgot about 'er."

Studying Bailey's deep green eyes for a long moment, Caleb rocked his jaw side to side, considering their options before he inquired, "Whatcha think?"

"I think we can't leave it there." Her brow furrowed that he would consider doing so. "Especially not with young. We need to get her some place warm and get a meal in her belly."

"All right," he agreed reluctantly, moving up the narrow path once again. "Go inside the house an' get us a blanket an' a few towels. I don' suppose you know how many pups there are."

"No." She shook her head, shoving her hands in her pockets. "It's too dark, and they're all curled in a ball."

By the time they had covered the short distance, the wind had begun to howl, and flakes were swirling around them like mad. Leading him to the end with the hole, she pointed. "In there."

"Go get the stuff." He wafted his hand towards the door while beginning to kick the slats next to the hole to break them.

"What're ya doin' that for?" Carson demanded, dismayed by the damage they would have to repair.

"We don't have time to crawl in there an' be all civilized. Besides, if she's been under there this whole time, we need t' get her out quick." Having completed removing about three feet of the wooden covering, he knelt down as Bailey returned. "Hello, mama," he called to the eyes that glared at him, noting that she began swooshing her tail slowly when he did so.

"Push the blanket in to me an' hold the towels," he commanded, sliding closer. "Does she have a name?"

"I think 'er name's Patches." Carson nodded as he spoke.

"Hey, Patches." Caleb shook his head as soon as he said it. *If she's only been here a few weeks, she ain't gonna know that's her name, but it's all I got.* Keeping his voice low, he continued to speak while stroking her thick fur. After a few minutes, he exhaled loudly, relieved that she didn't attack him when he touched her. Petting her, he worked to build her trust before he reached beneath her to remove her pups, one by one, three in all. "Toss me a towel!"

Catching the smaller portion of material, he spread it out slightly over the blanket, grasping each of the warm little bodies and grouping them in the center. Folding the edges over and sliding back towards the expanded entrance, he passed the parcel to the girl's waiting hands. "Wrap them in the other towel as well an' take them t' the house, little bit. Make a bed in the kitchen, close t' the oven so she can warm up. She's in bad shape."

Taking the bundle, Bailey moved quickly to obey, while Carson awaited his orders. Sliding back to the mother, Caleb worked the blanket beneath her, noticing how weak she appeared and that she did not even bother to resist. Once he had her encased in the thick comforter, with only her nose and face exposed, he began dragging her to safety.

"Go get the bottles an' stuff out o' the barn, Cars," he commanded.

"The ones for feedin'?"

"Yeah. Get them an' the nipples—the smallest we got." He made it out, hoisting the dog and pressing her against his chest. "She may not make it, but I think we should at least try to save her pups."

"Ok." The younger boy took off, disappearing into the wind-driven sheets of ice.

"Son of a bitch!" the older Cross cursed aloud to himself, lowering his face and turning down the road. The frigid air whirled around him, stinging his exposed flesh while he clutched the animal and fought his way to his home, where Bailey anxiously awaited.

Inside, the girl had kicked the oven on full blast, while laying the door open to allow the heat to flood the room. On the floor in front of it, she piled a quilt and clean towels for the pups, where she sat examining their tiny bodies. *They're so cute. There little eyes are scrunched shut, and they sound so adorable!*

"Is she ok?" She looked up at Caleb's entrance, wad of blanket and fur in hand.

"Too soon to call," he supplied, lowering the mother next to the bedding. Opening the covers, he used a fresh section of terrycloth to rub over the damp and chilled fur. "She needs warmth, water, an' food," he stated calmly, glancing at his brother when he entered the back door, carrying a crate of nursery equipment.

"I got it!" the youngster exclaimed, dropping the wooden box on the table and emptying his haul. "There's no milk, though."

"It's ok. We'll use the powdered," Caleb explained, shifting his gaze around the kitchen while scowling at its empty cupboards. "She can't eat this stuff, though." He surveyed the dry goods and cans that remained from their Midland stores. "We need to get some meat out o' Lawson—for her an' us."

Rising to peer out the window, Bailey pulled the blanket aside and glared into the white-out. "Man, it's really coming down."

"Yeah," he agreed, shifting the animal over onto the dry blankets and closer to the heat. "Cars an' I'll go get it. You start workin' on something warm for us to eat. We won' be long." With a wave of his hand, he and the boy passed through the portal and back into the storm.

Bailey leaned against the counter for a moment, staring at the wooden covering he had closed behind him. *He's a good man,* she considered him fondly, recalling all the times he had come to her rescue. *I'm lucky to have him in my life.*

Returning to the task at hand, she filled a pie pan with water and placed it on the floor next to the mother, which began to lap at the liquid greedily. "Well, I think that's a good sign." She petted her head softly.

Pulling out a large pot, she opened cans of vegetables and dumped them into water to boil for a stew. Then kneeling down next to her find, she returned to inspecting the puppies, noticing that they fit easily into her cupped hands, each with distinctive white, brown, or black markings. She was still messing with them, thinking about what their future might hold, when the back door opened and the young men clomped inside, stomping their feet to remove the snow caked on their boots.

"Here ya go," Caleb almost sounded jovial, placing his box on the table and holding up a jar. "All o' these have meat in them, an' we brought a ham."

"A ham!" the girl exclaimed. "From this summer?"

"I think so," he agreed, lifting the large round parcel that had been wrapped in thin cloth for storage. "We can eat for a few days on it, for sure." Opening one of the jars, he shredded some of the rabbit meat into a dish for the dog. "She's drinking. Tha's a good thing."

"Yes, I thought so, too," Bailey agreed, preparing their meal while he dealt with the animal.

On the floor next to him, Carson sounded disappointed. "All o' them are boys." He indicated the miniature bodies.

"How do you know?" the girl asked innocently.

"Are you serious?" He held the black and white one suspended for a moment while he gaped at her.

Feeling as if he were belittling her, she turned her back, busying herself with the dishes. Finally, she admitted, "Yes, I've never really been around animals before we came here. My mother didn't like the mess they make, so we never had any."

Rising next to her, Carson brushed his long bangs out of his eyes and offered her the small beast, spreading its hind legs. "See the li'l bump?" He indicated with a stiff finger. "Tha's boy parts. When he gets bigger, you'll see 'em better."

"Ah." She smiled, flicking her green eyes over at him. "Thanks."

"Don' mention it." He nodded, returning the pup to its mother, where the other two were trying to latch onto a nipple. "How old do you think they are, Caleb? They look perdy new t' me..." His voice trailed away as he poked them.

"A few hours," he replied, taking a chair with his food before him. "A day at most." He watched the girl, admiring her long auburn waves as she perched on the seat beside him. "If you hadn't found them, I don' think they woulda made it."

"Well, it was purely by accident that I did. I wanted to take care of the Knight house and heard the faintest of cries when I was going inside."

Carson joined them, sitting so he could watch the litter while the large female lay out and basked in the warm air. "What're we gonna call 'em?"

"It's too soon for names," Caleb interjected. "Give 'em a few days. If they make it, you can name them then." He shook his head, studying the lot. "An' don't feel so bad, little bit. We normally don' keep pets either."

"I've seen cats around here," she corrected, wondering where they had been hiding since the snowstorm had taken over the area.

"They're not pets. They keep the mice population down in the feed barn. Every animal on The Ranch serves a purpose. None of them are just here for the hell of it. We haven't had dogs here since the only two that were around when I was little died." He grimaced, moved by the memory of his childhood companions. "I guess that sounds pretty crazy, huh?"

"Not really, I guess." She shrugged while considering their newest members. "She found her way here, so I guess she belongs."

Caleb grinned at the young woman next to him. "Yeah, looks like we're takin' in more an' more strays every day."

Cutting her eyes over at him, she suppressed her own smile, fully aware he referred to her. "I didn't ask to be brought here," she retorted, "at least not last summer. But I'm very glad and grateful to be here now."

"We're glad you are too, Bailey-girl." His fingers tickled the back of her hand for a moment, then returned to the meal. Deciding he couldn't leave it at that, he teased, "Besides, if I hadn't been in Midland with you, I'd be missing along with everyone else. That's one good thing." He pointed his flatware at her. "An' you can cook, too. That makes you a keeper."

Bailey giggled loudly. "Well, at least I'm good for something," she tossed at him, wondering if that would be enough once the other women had returned to their sanctuary.

Devon frowned at the snow swirling outside their new window. "Can you believe dis shit?"

Amanda moved around the tiny apartment, poking and

searching the meager furnishings of their accommodations. "Have you figured out how we're gettin' outta here?"

"We still workin' on dat." He dropped the curtain, moving to slide his arms around her waist. "But it'll be soon. I promise ya."

Spinning in his grasp, she placed hers around his neck, pressing their lips together. "I love you, Dev," she cooed, her heart fluttering at the admission.

Stroking her long blond strands, his own joy overcame his concern for their situation, if only for a moment. Pressing his body more firmly against her, he growled. "Don' get too comfterble here."

"I won'." She grinned, dropping her arms and returning to her snooping. "Is there anything I can do t' help?"

"Jus' be ready." He nodded, pulling his coat on. "Gonna go meet up wit da others at th' diner. I'll bring you back a plate, an' you can stay here an' be warm wit th' babe." He smiled down at their infant, his finger tracing the line of her scalp while her name danced around in his mind. *Hope. Dat's what she is, all right.*

"Be back soon," he called, exiting and closing the door quietly behind him. Squinting into the storm, he shuffled his way through the gusts, arriving at the cafe a short time later. Removing the gloves and heavy jacket, he hung them on the hooks next to the door. Selecting a booth, he sank down onto the leather cushion and ordered coffee while he waited for the others.

A few minutes later, Don arrived and slid into the seat facing him. "We have a problem," he began without preamble.

"What's it now?" Devon's large black hands encircled his cup.

"We're gonna have t' kill the guards in the jail if we wanna get all our people out. That's one thing. But…" He hesitated, his eyes darting around the small space while dropping his voice even further. "I don' think we can wait a week. There may be a trial in a day or two, an' I don't like our chances o' what they may get sentenced to."

"Yeah," Devon agreed, sipping loudly. "Crazy buncha fucks

here. Can you get 'em out tonight? An' don' worry 'bout their losses. Some o' dem's gonna die."

"Sure, whenever." The other man grinned. "Got it all worked out. Just give me the word."

"Le's see how Luis is doin' wit our young-uns. Den we kin decide."

Ordering their meals, with a third to go for Amanda, the pair continued to wait until Luis came in from the cold, shaking off the snow and calling loudly to the waitress, "Hey there, Bonny Lass."

"I asked you not to call me that." The girl shook her ebony curls and grinned at her new friend. "Want your usual?"

"Sure." He took a seat at the counter to continue their banter, giving her a wink.

When his food arrived, she placed it before him. Leaning over from the other side, she breathed softly, "How's it you're over here with me while your friends are off over there?"

"Come on, Bonny." His face flushed slightly. "You think anyone knows about us?"

"They will if you keep hangin' around." She touched his hand lightly, indicating the other two men with a toss of her wrist. "Go sit with your friends. I'll see you tonight."

Taking his plate, he gave her another wink and obeyed her command. Pulling a chair over and taking the end of the booth, he drawled, "Fine weather we got here."

"You bangin' dat girl?" Devon accused in a hushed voice.

"Sure am," Luis agreed. "She may come in handy soon enough."

"Yeah, about that," Don countered, "we need to get outta here sooner rather than later. You got your part lined out?"

"Almost. I got all but two o' the girls located, an' gettin' 'em will be doable. But…" He paused, staring at Devon for a moment. "I can't find the boys. Can't go around asking too loudly, either, without drawin' suspicion."

"We cain't go without 'em." Devon pouted slightly. "Dat girl's over at The Ranch. She'll be expectin' them t' be wit us." Peering over his friend's shoulder, he watched the dark-haired waitress for a moment. "Does she know where dey's at?"

"No. I already asked her." Luis continued to devour the meal. "But I have an idea. We can take a few o' their people with us, kinda hold 'em for ransom, an' try to get the others back as a trade."

"That's a stupid plan," Don piped up. "You really think that shit'll work?"

"It's all we got." The other man furrowed his brow. "If you wanna go now, we gotta make some choices. You don't like my plan, gimme a better one."

The youngest of the trio only scowled, cutting his eyes over at the girl while she busily helped the few other patrons who had braved the storm to be there. "We can't wait. Besides, this mess outside'll be good cover for us to get away in. It'll make them think twice about comin' after us, too." Addressing his darker-skinned companion, "How do you know they're there?"

"Got a message." Devon grinned. "Dat red-headed girl sent it out, prolly to all o' us on her friends list. 'Course, I only had a few minutes while th' nurse was away from her computer, so I couldn't do much. An' 'Manda's outta da hospital now, so there's nothin' else we can do 'cept assume dey's still there an' things are good on that end."

"Fair enough." Don nodded. "We use the storm for cover, an' we go tonight." He indicated the jail that lay down the road. "We can't see it, but you know what I'm talking about."

"Yup." Luis pushed his empty plate aside. "We rally at ten tonight, after most o' the town's in bed asleep."

"Sounds good." Devon indicated he was ready to leave, taking the to-go box with him. "Soon as we get dem out, we'll get on t' gatherin' th' rest. Right now, I need t' make a few stops, take care o' few things 'fore I goes home."

Once he was gone, Don turned to the other man. "You really think we can pull this off? It's a fuckin' blizzard out there!"

"I know." Luis rubbed his chin.

"Well, if you're serious about takin' that girl, you better'd not say anything until the last minute. We don' wan' her warnin' anyone before we can make it outta here."

"Roger, chief." Luis stood, giving the young woman a small wave after he had pulled his jacket and gloves back into place. "See you around, Bonny Lass," his voice filled the small space.

The girl only grinned at his back as he exited through the glass entrance, her mind already lost on what he would do to her when they were alone together later that night.

SIX

Midnight Flight

AMANDA RAN her fingers firmly over the ebony flesh that covered his ribs. "It's no fun bein' your wife when we can't fuck," she complained, producing a small pout.

"You jus' had a baby." He laughed at her. "In a few weeks, you'll be ready t' get back in da saddle." He caught her fingers, toying with them for a moment before rolling over and pinning her beneath him. "An' after dat, we gonna get busy ev'r day."

"You bet we are." She giggled, kissing him lightly while her fingers caressed the smooth skin along his back. "We all set for tonight?"

"Yeah." He released her, standing to get dressed. "Get Hope all bundled up. It's still perdy cold, even without da wind an' da snow. I'll be back t' get you soon as da others are on der way."

"You know this plan o' yours really scares me," she admitted quietly while sliding into her jeans.

"Don' think about it, babe," he commanded. "Jus' do what you gotta do, an' don' be 'fraid. Bein' scared only makes it worse."

"'K." She nodded, sniffling slightly as she pulled her shirt over her head. "You should git. They'll be waitin' on you." Her blue eyes were misty when she peeked at him before he closed the door.

Slinging a large trash bag over his shoulder, Devon peered into the swirling flakes, noting that most of the structures were pitch black around him. Crossing the compound, he met Don and Luis behind the jail, the two of them huddling in the shadows to get clear of the wind, as well as out of sight.

Without comment, he walked past, and they fell in behind, headed around to the front entrance. Their attack a complete surprise, they didn't really expect any resistance and appeared calm when they cleared the glass door.

"Hey, fellas." The officer on duty grinned. "Kinda late for a visit, don't you think?"

"We ain't here for a visit." Don produced a pistol, shoving it towards the smaller man in uniform. "An' this don't have to end bad for you. Get your hands up!"

Lifting his palms slowly, his face crinkled. "What the hell are you guys doin'? A jail break in the middle of a blizzard? You must be a special kinda stupid…" His voice trailed away.

Taking offense, Devon stepped forward. Using the butt of his own weapon to crack the man's skull, he watched him fall to the ground. Glaring at him, he shoved the muzzle into the back of his head and executed him, his face placid as the man's blood leaked out, forming a puddle on the floor. Snatching the ring of keys off the hook behind the desk, he led the others down the hall.

Arriving at a short passageway lined on both sides with cells, he flashed his white teeth in the dim light. "Check da rest o' da buildin'. Kill anyone you find."

"Yes, sir," Don clipped, moving to the end of the hall. Locating no other people, he began gathering the weapons he found in what appeared to be the armory, calling loudly, "Damn. These guys don' even have this shit locked up!"

"That's good!" John joined him, relieved to be free but concerned about their next move. "I hope you boys've got more of a plan than this, though."

"We do." Luis grinned, pulling out boxes of ammo and putting them in his jacket pocket. "They got two four-wheel drive SUVs parked out back, an' we're gonna pack one of 'em with all this. You got it, Don?"

"Yeah. We're good."

"All right, you guys take care of this, an' I'll go hand out the kid assignments." Leaving the men to loading the weapons, he made his way down the hall and back to the lobby where the others had gathered. The group dug through the pile of coats that had been dumped on the floor, and some of the women began to cry.

"Where are my girls?" Paula demanded loudly, wiping at her tears.

"Relax, Mom," Devon addressed his new mother-in-law firmly. "'Manda's at home, gettin' our babe ready ta go, an' we'll get th' others 'fore we leave town."

"And why are we doing this now?" Peter demanded loudly, observing the snow for the first time. "We've been locked up for days. What would've a few more hurt?" He glared at the taller man, who appeared to be in charge of the rescue.

"Couldn' wait no longer. Things 're bad, an' only gonna get worse," Devon defended, noting that everyone had secured some kind of winter protection, although the fit was not ideal on most of them. "Sorry 'bout the sizes. It's the best we could do."

"Forget about that," Michael Small cut in. "What's the plan?"

Pulling out a pack of folded pages, Luis removed the rubber band and began handing them to the remainder of the men. "Each o' these is a location to one or more of our members. You go, break in, and I use that term loosely, because most o' the houses are not locked, an' you steal them back. If anyone wakes up or tries to stop you, kill 'em. We're gonna set fire t' the jail here at midnight. By then, you need to be at your location, loaded, an' ready to leave town, if not before."

"You have transportation for all of us?" Deanna appeared doubtful.

"We got a few trucks lined up. You girls are gonna help load up a few of our animals an' stuff. That's your job over the next two hours. Jus' remember most o' the town's asleep, so no loud noises.

If you have to talk to anyone, keep it down. No screamin' or racket."

"Yeah, like anyone's gonna hear us over this wind." Pete tossed a thumb over his shoulder to indicate the swirling storm while claiming the downed man's coat for his own. "Are we set?" He grinned at the folded sheet in his hand. "I like the little maps there, Luis. Nice work."

"I wasn't figurin' on you havin' to read 'em in the middle of a snowstorm." He grimaced. "I really hope this works."

"Not a jab, man." Peter nodded. "If this is our best shot, we need to make the most of it." Returning to the door, he pulled the hood of his jacket over his head and made his way out to get started on his part of the agenda.

Continuing to get everyone organized on their task, Luis remained at the police station until everyone had been dispersed. Pulling his own gloves and jacket into place, he headed towards the ranch house on the back side of the large community. *A whole fucking mile,* he grumbled to himself. His thoughts turned while he moved, his mind caught up in the ebony-haired beauty that would be waiting for him.

You shouldn't o' gotten personal, he admonished himself while bracing against a particularly strong gust of wind. Of course, it had been hard to avoid, since the girl was the daughter of his intended target. *We need those horses,* he reminded himself. *And if she gets hurt in the process, that's just how the cookie crumbles.*

Arriving at the gate a short time later, he let himself in and fought his way to the barn. Making his way down the stalls, he greeted each of their ponies, including the young foal that had been promised to the Dewitt boys. Stroking the small face for a moment, he thought about the two young men they had not been able to locate since their arrival in Pouty. *I wonder what they did with them.* He pondered their fate while he began loading the animals into the trailer located under the covered end of the building.

Placing Star in next to his mother and tying him off, he tossed a blanket across the smaller body. "Sorry, little buddy, but we gotta get home somehow." Leading the last few into the vehicle and securing the door, he glared at the house. *Moment of truth.*

Part of him wanted to leave the family undisturbed—steal the horses back, along with the truck and trailer, and be done with it. But in the end, he knew he couldn't do that. He would have to take care of the man inside, one way or another, and retrieve the girl.

Reaching the back door, he tried the handle, chuckling when it swung open easily. "Silly bastards," he mumbled, walking lightly across the linoleum and down the hall. Arriving at the master suite, he noted the entrance stood open, and he stepped inside. The room remained quiet, the silence only broken by the deep breaths of the slumbering couple.

Standing over them, he observed them for a long moment before changing his mind. Retracing his steps, he located Bonny's room easily enough and closed her door quietly behind him when he entered. The girl was also asleep, having returned home a few hours ago, after their rendezvous. His hand clamping over her mouth to prevent her from crying out, he woke her with a firm shake.

"Bonny Lass," he whispered loudly when her eyes fluttered, and she stopped struggling. Releasing her, he smiled. "Surprise!"

"What the hell are you doing here?" she cried, making the effort to keep her voice down. "Are you wanting my father to shoot your ass?"

"No, love." He caressed the cheek he had been holding. "But I don' wanna kill him, either."

She blinked at him from her reclined position. "Whadda ya mean, *kill him, either?*"

"I can't explain right now." He grabbed her covers, pulling them back and wishing he could join her beneath them instead. "I need to know if you wanna come with me." A mild panic gripped him at the thought she might say no.

Frowning, she climbed off the pliable surface, groggy at having been awakened from a sound sleep. "What the hell are you talking about, Luis?"

"We're leavin'," he supplied, gathering clothing for her to put on. "You have to decide if you're comin' with me." He handed her the items while she stood gaping at him. "I really want you to come, Bonny. I wasn't sure until just now, but yeah, I wanna take you with me."

She returned his gaze for a full minute, considering his words. Finally, she found her voice. "You guys weren't really joining us, were you?"

"No." He shook his head. "We got everyone busted out of the jail, an' we're takin' off. Put your clothes on and come with us."

"You want me to leave my parents and friends...and everything, just like that?"

Rolling his tongue for a moment, he eventually nodded. "Yeah. If you'll have me."

Her mind racing, the girl glanced at the door, realizing if she called out, her parents probably wouldn't hear her, and she would definitely incur the wrath of the man before her. "Ok. Let me get dressed." She began fumbling for the rest of her attire. When she was fully clothed, the couple exited the room, and she followed him out to the back, where she gathered her winter outerwear from a hook.

Making their way to the barn, she gasped. "You're stealing the horses?"

"Hey," he growled. "They were our horses. Your people stole them from us first."

Clamping her jaw shut, she looked around, aware that he had come alone. "Where's everyone else?"

"Gathering other stuff. We're leaving shortly." He glanced at his watch to check their time. "I need to pick up a few people, an' we're on our way."

"And where are we going, exactly?" she demanded.

"Back to The Ranch," he soothed, starting the truck and easing it around in the dark the best he could without the lights. Not seeing any sign of life from inside the house, he heaved a sigh of relief. "Stay warm, baby, an' I'll be right back."

Stepping out, he grinned at hitting the spot perfectly and attached the trailer easily in the dim light. Back inside the cab a few minutes later, he could tell the engine had warmed, as heated air spewed from the vents. Taking the road slowly, he eased them out onto the main thoroughfare.

Bonny stared at her family's home, still engulfed in darkness. *Damn.* "You didn't hurt them, did you?" Her voice small, it had occurred to her that he might have killed them all before coming to her room.

"No, baby." He shook his head. "Your family is fine." Pausing, he slowed the vehicle even more. "You wanna get out? I don' wanna take you if you don' wanna come."

Turning her gaze to him, she swallowed hard. "They won't forgive me for going with you."

"Then hop out." He flicked his fingers at her door while bringing the truck to a complete stop. "It's ok." He stared straight ahead.

Studying his profile for a moment, she thought about what her life had been like, living with her family in the midst of the group. *Going with him won't be much different.* Reaching over her shoulder, she grabbed her seat belt. "You should get moving. We don't want to be here if they wake up."

Grinning brightly, he agreed, "You got that right," while he eased their speed up and made his way a few houses down. Stopping, he watched the flakes pounding the glass for a moment before catching sight of a few figures moving in the darkness. Opening his door, he climbed out, allowing Nung and his three female companions to squeeze into the back seat.

Closing the half door behind them, he sighed in relief. "Everything go ok?"

"Good enough," Nung agreed, smiling at the blanket-clad girls. "Are we waiting or we goin'?"

"We go," Luis supplied. "Everyone is securing their own transport, and we're all going to the same place. We'll see them soon enough, if everyone makes it."

The group rode in silence while he expertly guided the massive load across the fresh snow. Making it to the main road, he eased around the turn and flicked on the headlights, placing them on dim. "Man, this's crazy, all this shit." He wafted a hand at the front glass.

No one replied, and he struggled to maintain his focus, again feeling a wave of relief when they reached the turn that led to their own fortress. It took the better part of an hour to make the last leg. Pulling through the mangled gate, he hoped they had been right about things being put back in order. He felt certain none of the others would allow his new companion into Lawson if they weren't.

Passing by the diner, he could make out the large pieces of plywood that covered the front glass. "Well, someone's here." A little further down the road, he could see the soft glow of the windows, the coverings dampening them but not completely. Parking at the end of the front porch, he called loudly, "Everybody out!" and dashed up the steps to beat on the door and find out exactly who it was that awaited their arrival.

SEVEN

Home Fires Burning

"BAILEY!" Caleb called her name, shaking her violently.

"What?!?" She pushed at the man hovering over her. "What's going on?"

"I need you t' get up." He laid his rifle across the couch and began pulling out pistols. "There's a car on the road."

"A car!" Carson leapt to his feet, making it to the window and pushing the blanket out of the way.

"Here, Cars, take this!" He wafted a long weapon towards the boy. "We don' know who it is yet, so we need t' be cautious."

"Why'd you turn the lights on then?" he demanded loudly.

The older male leaned against the window as well, watching the truck pull up in front of their home. Able to make out a horse trailer behind it, he swore loudly, "Son of a bitch! It's us!" Darting over, he flicked on the porch light and tossed open the door. Grabbing his jacket, he felt the cold air on his bare chest. "Hey!" he greeted Luis at the steps.

"Hey yourself." The older man offered him a hand to shake. "I got a truck full o' women here." He indicated the brood who were exiting the vehicle. "Mind if we drop by?"

"Not at all," the tall blond beamed. "Get inside, girls. Bailey'll get you somethin' warm for your bellies. You got our horses in there?"

"Yeah, most of 'em at least." Luis turned on his heel, sinking into the drifts up to his knees. "Is the barn ready?"

"Sure is. Gimme a sec, an' I'll ride over with you an' help get 'em unloaded." In a flash, he made it back inside, pulling off the jacket and tossing on a shirt. "You take care o' these guys, little bit?"

"Yes, sir." She saluted with a smile, giving Nung a nod. "You staying with us or going with them?"

"Well, we aren't all going to fit in here, not once the others arrive. How's the ranch house?"

"All set to go." She indicated the tall structure through the wall that lay between them. "All the beds are made, but you'll need to turn the heat up. It's only about fifty-five in there right now."

"Fair enough." He indicated the younger man. "Drop me off on your way to the stables, and I'll get the house ready."

Outside, the three men loaded into the vehicle and eased down the dirt path that ran between the greenhouse and the orchard. Letting Nung out at the driveway, Luis and Caleb arrived at the barn a short time later. While they unloaded the horses, neither of them bothered to speak; the howling wind would have made the effort impossible, and each of them wanted to get the task accomplished quickly as well.

Back at the Cross residence, Bailey put on a pot of coffee and inquired softly, "Anyone hungry?"

"No. I think we're all fed," Lacy Burns replied, reaching for a cup. "Just exhausted." Eyeing the slender young woman with ebony locks, she did not mince words. "Who the hell are you?"

Caught off guard by the blunt demand, Bonny stammered, "I'm...Luis' girlfriend." She overstated her position slightly, rubbing her hands on her jeans to warm them while she looked around. "I work over at the diner," she offered a bit more.

Shifting the focus to the other girls, Bailey queried, "How about you girls? You want something to eat?"

"No. We're good too." Kristen scowled, displeased that their number of extra females seemed to be growing.

"All right then. Well, the bathrooms are open and clean if anyone wants a shower. And the master bedroom is unoccupied if anyone needs to get some sleep." She indicated the stairs with an open palm.

Noticing the sound of whimpers, she turned her attention to their afternoon's distraction. "What's the matter, Patches?" On her knees, she gave the dog a few strokes before the other women noticed her curled up in the corner of the kitchen.

"Oh, wow," Jennifer commented loudly. "Is that Kimber's dog?"

"I guess so." Bailey shifted over so she could join her. "I found her under the Knight porch this morning, before the storm blew in again." Lifting a leg, she exposed the three tiny pups.

"My gosh! She has babies!" Kristen observed.

Leaning over to peer at them with a scowl, Lacy took charge of the situation. "All right, girls, it's very late, an' we need to figure out where everyone is going to be staying. What are the other structures like?"

Bailey stood slowly, stretching to her full height so that she could look down at the slightly shorter woman. "We've been working on them, if that's what you mean. The guys boarded up all the windows, and I was in the process of cleaning things out and getting them ready for your return."

"An' just how did you know we were coming back?" Her brown eyes narrowed into thin slits.

"Devon replied to my message." The girl felt confused. "Look, I don't know what you're accusing me of, but I assure you, I'm as much a part of this community as you are!"

Bonny shifted uncomfortably. "I guess I'll take a cup of coffee," she offered, hoping to break the tension between the other two women.

Pausing the argument to locate a cup for her, Bailey pulled out several, placing them on the counter. "Help yourself." She took the opportunity to return her attention to the dog, which had begun to whimper more loudly. "What's the matter, girl? Time for another trip outside?"

They had already established that the dog did not like making a mess in the house and, despite the cold, preferred to venture out when nature called. Pulling open the back door, she spoke cheerily, "Here you go, girl," and Patches immediately got to her feet, leaving her babies in the blanket while she wandered outside. Making it quick, she clawed at the door a few minutes later, and Bailey let her back in, giving her a scratch behind the ears. "Such a good girl!"

Having served themselves cups of warm liquid, the group gathered around the kitchen table, while Carson called from the front room, "There's another car on the road!"

Immediately, a small chaos ensued, as the girls fluttered about and prepared to greet the next group of arrivals.

Frowning at the mattress in the living room floor, Lacy commanded, "Carson, can we get this back upstairs where it belongs?"

"Yes, ma'am," he replied dejectedly, pulling the bedding off the top and tossing it aside.

"Here," Bailey interceded. "Let's lean it against the wall for now. You can take it back up when your brother gets back to help." She didn't like the way the other woman had taken over things. *Giving orders like she owns the place.*

With the porch light on, the next vehicle had easily identified the group's location. It turned out to be a pickup truck with four people crammed in the single cab and the back laden with cages.

"Oh my God." Lacy darted out the door, recognizing her oldest daughter.

Dashing out into the crisp night air right behind her, Bailey noticed that the wind had died down. Grabbing her uncle, who had driven the second transport, she demanded loudly, "Where's the boys?"

"Not with me," he clipped. "They'll come. Right now, I need to get these rabbits inside before they freeze to death." He lifted a corner of the tarp that held the snow off their cages.

"The barn's all set," she supplied, blinking back tears. "Carson, go help get them squared away, please."

As soon as that vehicle had moved out, a third pulled in, only this time they parked across the street, in front of the armory. Climbing out, John gave a wave, opening the back door so that two of the Smalls and Connie Fox could exit. Joining the larger group of women in short order, the older woman took over, demanding to know many of the same things Lacy had been informed of.

Leading the group inside, Bailey started a second pot of coffee, her hands trembling while she did so. "Do any of you have word on my brothers?" she asked in a calm voice, hoping to cover her raw emotions.

"They'll be along, child," Connie offered, giving the girl a hug, which surprised Lacy as much as it did Bailey.

Allowing the oldest woman in their community to hold her for a moment, she sobbed, "What if they don't? I can't bear the thought of losing them!"

"It'll work out," the matriarch reassured, giving her hair a stroke with her knobby fingers. "Right now, we need t' get settled in."

Moving to obey, the girl continued to play hostess to each new group of arrivals by helping to keep the coffee made. Another group arrived, and she struggled to hide her disappointment that her brothers were not among them.

Eventually, Nung returned to announce the ranch house was ready. At his suggestion, the majority of them would move to the larger structure, where they could spread out and get some rest until sunrise. Dividing up, everyone who would be relocating loaded into a vehicle, leaving Bailey and Peter behind with the two Crosses and their would-be hostage, should the need arise.

When Caleb and Luis came back from tending the horses and helping to get the rabbits back into their cages, the latter immediately located Bonny and swept her into his arms. Observing the couple, the tall blond grinned, giving Bailey a sideways glance and longing to do the same. Instead, he smiled his approval at her ability to handle herself, complimenting her in a quiet tone. "You did good, little bit."

Her eyes hollow, she gave no reply. Although she had held herself together thus far, the missing members of the community tore at her from the inside. Others may rest that night, but there would be no way for her to lay her growing feelings of loss aside.

Shaking his head, Pete wanted to suggest Bailey and he go with the larger group, but he knew the house would be crowded. *Besides*, he rationalized, *she'll want to remain here and wait for her brothers*. "John, why don't you guys go on down to the ranch house an' get some rest. I'll stay here with the kids and wait for the rest."

His best friend cast a wary glance around the small group, then reluctantly agreed. "Sounds like a plan. Luis, bring your woman, an' we'll see how things shape up at first light." Climbing into one of the remaining vehicles, they left the trio to await the last of their comrades.

Once they were gone, Peter sighed loudly. He had learned from Devon that the boys had not been located prior to their hasty exit. *It'll be nothing short of a miracle if they come in with one of the remaining groups*. However, he did not care to share that bit of news until the issue had been laid to rest, choosing to allow her to keep her hopes for their safe return.

Instead, he poured himself a cup of coffee and made his way over to inspect the dog that had been quietly observing the comings and goings of everyone from the corner. "Well, I see the mutt survived."

"Barely." Caleb joined him. "If Bailey hadn't heard her under the Knight porch today, I'm sure she'd o' been a goner." Grinning, he reached beneath her to produce a small brown handful of fur. "Lookie here." He handed the animal to her uncle.

"Oh, wow." Peter accepted the offering. "How many?"

"Only three." He massaged his chin roughly. "Been a long time since we had any dogs around here."

"Yeah," Pete agreed. "Maybe it's about time, too." Returning it to its warm bed, the pair rose and moved to the living area. "You guys been sleeping down here?" he asked calmly, eyeing the mattress leaned against the wall.

"That's for Bailey," Caleb quickly clarified. "I've been on the couch an' Carson on the chair." He pointed at the furniture to solidify his version of the situation.

Inhaling deeply, the older man cut his eyes over at him. "It's ok, son. I'm not mad. You guys've been together almost a year. That's longer than some marriages."

The color drained from Bailey's flushed cheeks. "What's that supposed to mean?" she stammered, shocked by the insinuation. "Caleb and I are just friends!"

Waving her off, the man in question shoved his hands in his pockets. "It's ok, little bit. I'm sure he's not the only one that has the wrong idea about us."

"Well, that's great." The color returned to her features in a flash of anger. "They can get that idea out of their heads." Spinning around, she stomped into the bathroom and slammed the door behind her, closing the lid to the toilet with a loud bang. Plunking down on it, she chose to hide in the only place of refuge she felt comfortable taking in the house that in no way belonged to her.

EIGHT

Let's Make a Deal

PETER WATCHED his niece disappear with his mouth hanging ajar. Using his right hand to push it closed by rubbing his stubble, he shifted his glare over to the younger man. "You bein' square with me?"

"Yeah, man. You see how she is." He flopped a hand after the moody female. "One minute, I think she's all hot for me, an' the next, she's givin' me the cold shoulder."

Pete broke into a wide grin, observing. "A bit confusing, isn't it?"

"Yeah...so I'm keepin' my distance. Safer that way." Caleb turned his back, glaring out the window towards the gate. "Where do you suppose the rest of 'em are?"

"I hate to think about it." The older man frowned. "The plan was to have everyone out of town by midnight. That was over an hour ago, an' I don't see how the weather could be the reason some of them didn't make it."

"Should we go check? Maybe retrace the path in case they're stuck somewhere along the way?"

"Let's give it a few more minutes." He flicked his gaze towards the room where his niece remained in hiding. "When she decides to rejoin us, we can decide."

"Hell, tha's easy enough." Caleb sauntered down the hall, beating quite loudly on the door. "Hey, princess, we need you out here."

Bailey had nearly fallen off the toilet at his harshly interrupting her thoughts. Hearing his demand, she made it to the door and stood toe to toe with him before he had finished speaking. "Princess now? I thought we were past all that!"

"Me too, but you seem to fall back into it every once in a while." He grinned as he teased her. "Pete thinks we can go check on the last of them, make sure they haven't gotten stuck."

"Sure!" she quickly agreed, her mind instantly on the twins.

Putting on her boots and grabbing coats, they were set and ready to face the cold that remained, even if the wind and snow had subsided. Following Pete, the three of them piled into their Jeep Wrangler, with Bailey taking the rear so the two men could sit up front.

Leaning back into the seat, the girl watched the diner slowly pass by her window, a sad feeling creeping over her at the sight of it. "It's a real shame they tore everything up so much."

"Yes," Peter agreed. "I was taken down right away, so I didn't get to see what all happened, but from what I was told once we were in the jail, our guys put up a good fight."

"Not good enough," Caleb countered, taking it easy as they cleared the gate.

"Well, not at the time," the other man agreed. "But I'm sure we made up for it tonight."

Bailey shuddered, his words giving her an ominous ache in the pit of her stomach. "What did you guys do to them?" When he didn't answer, she leaned her head against the glass and watched the ditch creep by in silence.

A moment later, Caleb gasped loudly. "Oh shit! Is that their helicopter?"

Peter pointed at the floating light in the distance. "Yup! Can you turn around?"

"Not gonna risk it." He stopped the vehicle and threw it in reverse. Placing his hand behind the passenger seat, he wedged himself so he could watch out the rear glass as he drove backwards, clearing the gate a few minutes later.

By that time, the aircraft had landed on their airstrip, and he turned left onto the road that lay next to the gate and ran the inner perimeter of the wall. Arriving next to the contraption, the blades had stopped spinning, and Devon exited the cabin.

Recognizing him, Pete jumped out, clasping his hand firmly. "You made it!"

"Yeah." His bright white teeth gleamed against his dark face. "Help me get dem in da car."

Peter obeyed, and a moment later, Amanda slid into the back seat next to Bailey, who kidded the other girl quietly, "Thanks for th' ride!" while pulling her baby to her more snugly.

Bailey stiffened slightly, not returning the blonde's grin. Her gaze dropping to the bundle of blankets that rested against her chest, she demanded, "Where's everyone else?"

Kathy slid into the passenger seat next to Caleb and said firmly, "When we get inside, we'll share. Right now, we need to get warm."

Seeing that Peter and Devon were occupied, Caleb put the vehicle into drive and eased it on around the twisted path, arriving at his home with his new cargo a few minutes later. Climbing out and entering through the kitchen, Kathy made sure that Amanda and the newborn were inside, ushering her up the stairs and into the master bedroom.

Choosing not to follow, Bailey had entered the house behind them, sinking limply into a stiff kitchen chair. Sensing her distress, Caleb knelt before her, peering up into her glazed green orbs. "Bailey," his soft voice broke the silence.

Shaking her head slowly, she spoke hoarsely, "They didn't bring my brothers."

"I'm sure they're ok," he lied flatly, gripped by his own fears, his mother being among those who had not returned. His hand grasping her knee, he squeezed. "We'll get the details shortly," he reassured.

Meeting his gaze, the girl had no will to resist the darkness that clouded her thoughts. She had lost so much in the last year; these last two would surely break her completely. Her face contorted, the sound started as a low moan, quickly escalating into a high-pitched wail.

Rising, Caleb pulled her to her feet. Slowly removing her stocking cap, he applied pressure to her scalp. His arms wound tightly around her, her body shook, her gasping howls unchecked.

Clenching her fists, she pounded heavily on his broad shoulders, succumbing to her anguish. Then clinging to him tightly, she sobbed, "They're gone, Caleb! My baby brothers are gone!"

Unable to disagree, tears leaked from his eyes, his fingers woven into her tresses, tracing the nape of her neck. "Don't say that, Bailey! Don' give up yet!"

The back door opened, and Peter clomped inside, Devon close behind. Noting the couple locked in an embrace, he demanded loudly, "What's happened?"

Releasing the girl enough to face them at an angle, Caleb demanded, "Where's everyone else?" He glared at Devon, his eyes icily accusing the tall black man of leaving them behind.

"Dey's still in Pouty," the other man confessed. "But we'll get 'em back!"

"Yeah? How!?!" Caleb removed his jacket and helped Bailey out of hers. "How could you guys leave them there?" He addressed both men, aware that they had made their escape together.

Peter kept his explanation short. "There were too many of us to get out together. We were all spread out, an' we had to split up. We did what we could. Your mother an' the boys, they're only part of those who are still over there, so don't worry. We *will* get them back." His eyes darting between his two accusers nervously, his own role in their plan felt foolish. "Bailey, don't worry, really. Not yet. We'll cut a deal—make a trade or something and get them back. I'm sure they won't hurt them."

Caleb frowned, his arm around the girl, pulling her firmly into his chest and holding her in a half embrace. He knew there was nothing they could do at the moment, and the odds of any such attempt being successful were slim. "What did you do to them?" he asked more quietly.

The color drained from Peter's face, no longer able to hold his front. "We got out. We did what we had to in order to escape." He paused, casting a glance over at the taller man next to him. "Did you guys complete the plan?"

"Yeah, only dey got Chris. He an' Martha didn' make it." He sighed loudly. "Far as the boys, we couldn't find 'em. An' two o' da girls was missin', " he confessed. "But we still get 'em back." He grasped Bailey's right shoulder, giving her a squeeze. "We got a few things t' trade for 'em."

"I can't believe you left without them." She glared at her uncle, refusing to be pacified.

"Shhshh," Caleb soothed, tightening his grip. "I'm sure they did what they could. Besides, there were a lot of lives at stake, an' most of 'em got away. Tha's really what counts."

Pulling away, she stared into his clear blue eyes. "You really believe that? They left your mother over there for Christ's sake!"

"I'm sure they had no other choice." He nodded at the two men.

Kathy joined the group at that moment and interrupted their pow-wow in an authoritative manner. "Devon, your wife is in John and Martha's bed, if you want to join her there. I can let you take Carson's room if you like." She wafted a hand at Peter. "Since I will fit better in the chair."

"That won't be necessary." Pete shook his head. "You go on an' take the bed, an' I'll stay down here with the kids. I guess we're all here, for now, an' we need to get some sleep. We'll need to get a lot of things done as soon as the sun comes up, getting that gate blocked being at the top of the list.

Devon guided the woman up the stairs, thanking her for taking care of his wife and child as they disappeared onto the second level. Bailey watched them with doleful eyes, her tears again streaming down her face.

Giving her another squeeze, Caleb led her over to her mattress, where he pushed her to sit and removed her boots for her. "Lay down, little bit," he instructed as he grasped the blanket and covered her shivering body, fairly certain her quivers were not a result of being cold.

"Lay with me," she begged quietly, her eyes wide pools of sorrow.

Pursing his lips, he studied her tear-stained face while considering the request. "Ok." He nodded, kicking off his own footwear and stretching out beside her, facing her as he had done in the car only a few nights before. "Take the couch, Pete," he called to the other man, who had been removing his own outer layer.

Stretching out on the cushioned surface, Peter sighed deeply, resting his arm across his forehead while he stared at the ceiling above him. *Damn.* He hated like hell that his two nephews were missing and only hoped to God they could in fact get them back.

NINE

No Room

THE EXHAUSTED GROUP fell into slumber quickly, only to be awakened a few hours later when John Cross came stomping through his house. Only glancing at the bodies that had begun to stir in his living room, he scowled at the sight of his son lying on a mattress, the Dewitt girl curled in his arms.

Continuing his ruckus, he clomped up the stairs to see who else had returned. He opened his bedroom door and closed it quickly in front of his own face, having discovered a couple in his bed. "Devon?"

"Yeah, whattcha need?" the large black man called while sitting up slowly, trying not to disturb the young blonde lying next to him.

"We got work t' do," John stated loudly through the wood. "Get your family together an' bring 'em down t' th' ranch house quick as you can. We got food an' a place for them there with the other women an' children."

Returning to the hall, he knocked on Carson's door before opening it and called through the crack, "Who's in here?"

"Kathy," the woman replied. "I'm decent, John." She sat up on the bed, still fully dressed.

"Tha's good." He stepped inside. "Breakfast's at the ranch house." He nodded to their medical staff and closed the door behind him. He then made his way to the stairs to rouse the rest of the crew if they hadn't made it to their feet already.

Inside the master's quarters, Amanda sighed loudly and rolled over. She slid out from the sheets, pulling their daughter to the edge to change her diaper and dress her tiny frame. Having only moments before completed their morning feeding, she smiled at how much lighter her breasts felt at the moment, amazed that she could make all the sustenance her infant needed, at least for the time being.

"Things're gonna work out, aren't they, Dev?" She turned to locate her own clothing.

"We'll be ok," he agreed. "Jus' need t' stick together. Get yurself ready, an' I'll take ya down like he said," he commanded, moving to the bathroom for a quick shower before he dressed to face the day.

Downstairs, Caleb had awoken when his father came through the room and lay staring at Bailey's sealed lashes when he returned.

"Get up," the older man instructed. "Get down t' the servin' line an' get fed. We got a full day o' work ahead o' us gettin' the walls blocked off 'fore those asshats come after us."

Peter was on his feet, already pulling on his jacket. "I don't know that we got the materials to block that gate off."

"We need t' tear down the arena," Caleb supplied. "That's what we decided before you guys got here. We didn' have the manpower t' complete it though," he lamented.

"Tha's th' plan," his father agreed, giving his boy a nod. "Le's move." His voice gruff, he shook his head to himself, making his exit and heading to the barn that housed the big CAT they would use to complete much of the process.

Running his fingers lightly along her jaw, Caleb caressed the female into consciousness. "Time to get up, little bit."

"What time is it?" she inquired in a soft voice, stretching at the same time.

"I dunno," he confessed, pushing himself up and getting to his feet. "It's still dark, so it's pretty early. I'll take care o' the dog, an' we'll get outta here. They got breakfast for us, an' then we got lots to do."

Giving no argument, the girl slipped into the bathroom to pee and to give her reflection a scowl in the mirror. *Sleeping in your clothes is becoming a bad habit.* Of course, she really didn't have any options at the moment either, as there was no room to spread out and have much privacy now that most of the community had returned. Washing her face to wake herself more fully, she exited the tiny room a few minutes later to discover Devon had joined them.

"We're gonna wait on 'Manda so we can all take the Jeep together," Caleb informed her. "Kathy rode with your uncle."

"Ok." She nodded her approval. "I'd like to check on the outside world if you don't mind." She wafted a hand at the small office.

"Naw," he agreed with a wave of his own towards the alcove. "We got a few minutes. See what's left out there, if you can."

Sliding into the chair in front of the computer, Bailey's heart began to pound out of control. Staring at the screen a few minutes later, she wished she had passed on her curiosity. Returning to the kitchen, she got right to the point. "We're fucked."

"Whadda ya mean by that?" Amanda demanded from the stairs.

"The whole world is caught up in this mess." Bailey could see the other girl was overloaded between her bag and infant and moved to help her by taking the luggage. Shuffling the heavy satchel over her shoulder, she grinned at her nemesis anxiously.

Caleb watched the girls nervously, kneeling to give the dog a pat. Wafting a hand, he indicated the back door. "Got the car warmed up for us. We can discuss it on the road," he stated flatly as he made his exit.

Following, the group piled into the Wrangler, the men taking the front seats while the girls took the back. Flicking her gaze over at the tall blonde, Bailey frowned. "The internet is still working, but not many people are using it. All of the stupid stories Yahoo always carried are gone. No *who's sleeping with who in Hollywood* nonsense scrolling across the page."

"So what're they saying?" Caleb eased the vehicle through the darkness, noting it had begun to snow lightly once again.

"Europe and Asia are getting dumped on, same as we are. And most of the northern states have gone dark. There's power outages from coast to coast that are days or weeks long now, and most of the cities are seeing riots, while everyone is scrounging for food. I guess FEMA can't really save us all, can it…" Her voice trailed away.

"No, little bit," Caleb's voice softened, "they can't save us all. How's Illinois?" He glanced at her in the rear-view mirror.

"Frozen," she whispered, staring out the portal to her left, causing him to once again regret his ice age comment from last summer.

"I'm sorry, Bailey," he soothed, pulling up behind the other parked vehicles.

"It's ok." She glanced at the girl next to her, eager to change the subject, enough to make peace with her enemy. "What's her name?"

Amanda smiled, hugging her babe more tightly as she climbed out. "Hope. We named her…Hope."

"That's a nice name." Bailey pulled the stocking cap from her head as they entered the familiar structure. Inhaling deeply, pangs of hunger flooded into her consciousness. "Man, Connie has been cooking up a storm!"

"Sure have, missy," the older woman teased. "While you's sleepin' in! Get yourselves served. We got a full day ahead, snow or no snow."

"Yes, ma'am." The girl flicked her auburn locks, taking a plate and joining the others.

Half an hour later, the entire company had been fed, and Luis took Bonny's hand. The couple would be heading over to the diner to get started setting it straight, and Bailey quickly realized it was actually to get the outsider out of the way while the real job assignments were handed out.

Most of the men would be taking care of dismantling the horse arena and using the materials to shore up the wall, completely sealing the main gate. Bailey and a few of the other girls would be visiting the rest of the houses, getting them back into shape so the families could return to their homes.

Finally, a few of the women were going down into Lawson, to begin prepping their quarters so the group could transition underground seamlessly if the need should arise. At hearing this, Bailey asked quietly, "Why don't we just go now? Lock ourselves in and hide?"

"Because," Pete supplied, "we still have to defend the surface. We need the structures for the animals an' the windmills that provide water and electricity for us. Besides, livin' down there would be really hard on morale. We need to maintain some semblance of normal for as long as we can."

The girl grimaced at the explanation, following him out onto the porch. "Hmmp, like all this snow is conducive to normal."

"Easy, Bailey-girl," he chided more quietly. "You're still on probation around here." He glanced at the few who had followed them. "Keep a positive attitude an' do what you're asked."

"I will," she agreed with a nod, making sure her hat and gloves were in place. "I guess we can pick up at the Knight's place," she informed the three girls who had been assigned to help her with the task. Leading the way, Kristen, Rebecca, and Amber followed close behind.

As soon as they were inside the second structure, Rebecca Burns grabbed the older girl by the shoulder, giving her a strong hug. "We're so glad you made it back here!"

Stunned, Bailey stared at the other girls, Kristen's shock at the move evident. "Well, I'm glad you guys made it out of Pouty. Only, I wish my brothers could have escaped, too."

"Don' worry," Amber reassured. "Our dad's still there, an' he'll look out for them!" She grinned at the tallest girl, having grown close to her through months of Facebook chat. "I know mom still don't think much o' you, but she'll come around."

"Thanks"—Bailey sighed—"I think." She flicked her eyes across their faces nervously. "Let's start here and work our way through the house and finish on the other end." Quickly going over the process she had been using to clean up the mess and get the space reorganized enough to make it livable, the group set to work. An hour later, they were ready to move on, the work much quicker with four sets of hands.

Outside, the sun had begun to break through the clouds, casting a soft grey glow across everything. Bailey had noted it was nearly nine, by the clock on the wall in the Knight kitchen, but the dark overcast made that hard to believe. Arriving at their next stop, the group surveyed the Burns' home in disgust.

"Jesus Christ," Rebecca swore loudly. "Those bastards tore up everything!"

"Yes." Bailey joined in her friend's displeasure. "It took me hours to clean up what they did to the Cross house. It almost looks as if they were after something, the way they pulled everything out and ransacked it."

"Maybe." Kristen frowned. "I guess this means my house is gonna look the same way?" She indicated the adjacent structure through the wall with an open palm.

"Pretty much." Their leader sighed. "No use crying over it, though. We need to gather everything up, and you guys can go through it later when you have time." Handing out the trash bags, she put an end to the discussion matter-of-factly.

Half an hour later, the group was still working on the living room and kitchen, when a horrific boom caused the small dwelling to shake. Bolting to the door, they moved to the porch, noticing that the big CAT had been overturned and lay on its side. Her eyes wide in horror, Bailey blinked rapidly, realizing what she was seeing through the haze—Caleb's body lying a few feet from the capsized machine.

TEN

Call Me Baby

THE CRY that escaped the girl sounded odd, almost foreign to her as she dashed across the snow. Her auburn locks whipping behind, her bare hands clutched at the prone figure, pulling at his jacket to roll him over. Coughing a few times, Caleb made it onto his knees, sitting back on his haunches and gasping to breathe. "I'm ok, little bit."

"Stop it," she commanded, her fingers finding their way to his face in the freezing air. Continuing to inspect him, she discovered that he appeared bruised, but all of his limbs were attached.

Catching her hands when his mind began to clear, he demanded, "Where the hell is your coat?"

"Still in the house, I guess," she stammered, still too stricken for rational thought.

"Come on." He stumbled to his feet, dragging her with him. Casting his gaze around the area, he noted the rest of the community had stopped moving, and everyone stood in a transfixed state, glaring at the couple. "Get your jacket," he instructed, indicating the porch where the rest of her crew stood gaping at them. "An' find Kathy for me. I'll be at the med center." He took two steps in that direction before he collapsed.

"CALEB!" she screamed again, dropping down next to him once more.

She still had a hold of him when one of the girls reached them and demanded, "Here, Bailey, put this on!"

Taking the protection against the cold, the girl slid her arms into the sleeves, her emotions running too high to really notice the bite of the wind. "We need help," she stammered.

"Kristen went to find Kathy," Amber supplied. "The guys are gonna get him to the med center." She indicated the two men who were approaching carrying a two by eight plank about eight foot long in length.

"He can't balance on that!" Bailey objected.

"Get a blanket from the house," Peter instructed the younger girl. "We'll use the wood as a brace an' carry him in a hammock."

A few minutes later, they were set, one man on each corner of the oversized cloth, lifting and sliding the injured Caleb lightly across the snow. The system worked perfectly, the board giving the setup a bit of structure so that he didn't become folded inside the comforter. Arriving at the med center a few minutes later, Kathy was already there and prepared to take charge.

Shooing the men and girls out of the building, only she and Bailey remained. "Can you stay and assist me?" she asked of her green-eyed companion without looking at her.

"Of course." The girl pulled off her coat.

"Good." Kathy forced a smile. "We need to get these clothes off and evaluate his injuries." She began by tugging at his jacket and rolling him onto his side to get it off of him. "We'll cut the rest," she stated flatly.

His eyes popping open, Caleb countered, "That won' be necessary."

"Oh my God." Bailey grasped his hair and shirt, laying her face on his broad chest.

"We have to remove these," the nurse insisted. "And I don't want you trying to stand until I've evaluated you," she stipulated.

"Ok," he breathed heavily, wincing at the shoots of pain each inhalation produced. Staring at the bright lights above him, he commanded, "Gimme a minute, an' I can get 'em off from here." Running his hand down her trembling back, he tried again. "Lemme up, little bit. I'm ok."

Her face stained with tears, the girl released him, taking a step back and folding her hands in front of her face. "Let me know if you need help." Watching his effort, she focused on calming her breathing, aware that her panic wasn't helping anyone.

"Sure." He smiled, cutting his eyes over at her. Fumbling with the buttons for a moment, he sighed loudly. "Ok, I need help."

The girl eagerly took charge. "Lay still." Unfastening the shirt, she helped him slide it off and lifted the white thermal underwear that lay beneath it, exhaling a loud gasp.

"It's ok," Kathy soothed, joining in by unclasping his pants and helping him to get them down. "He's responsive and moving around. That's a good sign."

A few minutes later, the pair of females had stripped the man to his tight cotton briefs, to which he announced, "Ok, I think tha's far enough. Whatta you think?"

Her fingers probing, the woman made her evaluation. Deciding she needed some X-rays, she instructed, "Bailey, I need you to wait outside. Only for a minute." She grinned at the girl's displeased countenance.

Obeying, Bailey made her way down the road to the Cross home, where she let the momma dog out and gave her fresh food and water. Then slipping upstairs, she gathered clean and dry clothing for Caleb and returned to the med center, where she found him sitting on the table while Kathy wrapped his ribs in brown strips of cloth.

"Well?" she demanded loudly.

"Cracked ribs," the man supplied, eyeing her bundle. "Those for me?"

"Yes." She grinned sheepishly. "I took care of the dog, too."

"Nice." He flinched. "Easy there, lady."

"Just sit still." She continued to prod him with practiced hands.

"You're a lucky man, Caleb Cross." Her eyes flicked over at the girl. "On two counts, I think." Finished with the dressing, she instructed him to stand so she could inspect him, which he complied on shaky limbs.

"All right," she gave her assessment a few minutes later. "You're off duty for at least forty-eight hours. Go home and get some rest, and if you have any new symptoms, no matter how small, you get me immediately. We're a long way from a real hospital, and timing will be critical if this turns out to be anything worse."

"Yes, ma'am," he agreed, reaching for the fresh clothing. "Any chance I could get a ride home?" His blue eyes wide, he hated to ask the girl to walk all the way to the ranch house to retrieve their vehicle, but there wasn't any other option. "I don't think the cart will be enough power in the snow…"

"Not at all!" she volunteered readily. "Get dressed, and I'll be back shortly with the Jeep." Darting out the door once more, she jogged through the knee- to thigh-high drifts the best she could, thoroughly exhausted by the time she reached the Wrangler and climbed inside.

Easing the vehicle over the path, she arrived back at the med center and helped him climb into the passenger seat. "It hurts," she stated flatly, noting the lines drawn deeply into his face.

"Yeah," he agreed with a pant. "But I'm alive."

His words caused her eyes to sting, and she blinked rapidly as she slid behind the wheel. Parking next to the back door a few minutes later, she helped him out and up the back steps. Getting him settled on the couch, she wiped at the drops that had escaped and moistened her lashes.

Catching her hand, he grinned up at her, preventing her escape. "It's ok, Bailey. Really, I'm fine."

Staring into his clear blue orbs, she let the flood gates swing wide, the tears streaming down her flushed cheeks. "I was so scared!"

"I know." He pulled at her, working her legs to either side of his hips so that she straddled him, sitting in his lap in a completely awkward and suggestive position. Their faces only inches apart, he ran his hands up and down her back, soothing her while she tried to stem the flow. "I guess you're not really my best friend anymore."

"What the hell is that supposed to mean?" She sniffled.

His grin slow, like a morning sunrise, it spread across his face and warmed her heart. "I think we're beyond that now," he professed. Pulling her to him, his lips touched her gently, suctioning lightly to hers for a moment before he parted them, allowing his tongue to explore and taste her more fully.

Beginning to tremble, Bailey settled into the affectionate act, the lump pressing into her groin adding fuel to her fire. Lifting her mouth, "Oh my God, Caleb," she breathed, her fingers pushing through his short blond strands. Placing her cheek against his, her chest contracted, forcing her breaths into eager pants.

"Easy, little bit." He grasped her ribs a moment later, manipulating a small space between their bodies before his hands slid up to brush briefly across her mounds. "We need to keep a lid on this. At least for the time being."

Staring at him, his words hardly made sense. "Why?"

"Because you promised, that's why." He leaned forward, ignoring the pain the movement produced, to nuzzle her neck. "An' when I'm all better, I'm gonna have you." His warm air tickled her flesh. "An' it's gonna be perfect."

His words sent shivers down her spine, his hands on her only adding to the blaze that had begun to burn, the moist heat growing urgent where their bodies remained pressed together.

"Oh, shit," she breathed, biting at his ear, fingers still filled with hair she pulled on firmly. "I want you, Caleb! Do you have any idea how long or how badly?"

Releasing her, he slid his hands along her arms, clasping her fingers to free his head from her grasp. "Yeah, baby, I know! But it's not time yet." He pushed her back, overpowering her resistance. "We'll get the chance. Don't worry." He studied her green pools intently. "I said don't worry. I'm gonna have you. Jus' not today."

Giving her a firm shove, he pushed her off of him, feeling torn the moment the cool air covered his lap where she had been sitting. It would have been so easy to let go of those ideals and strip her down right then and there. *But we've waited too long to give it up now,* he reminded himself once more. Peering up at her disappointed features, he half-smiled. "Make me sumthin' to eat?"

Her hand grazing his jaw, she grinned at the roughness of his stubble, her raw need still raging inside. Blinking at him a few times, she knew in her heart that he was right and they should wait, but her body's desire to be taken made it so hard to comply. A full minute later, she whispered, "Call me baby again."

"What?" he stammered, thrown off by the odd request.

"Call me baby," she demanded a little more firmly. "It's the first nickname you've given me that I actually like." Her grin spread wide, exposing her perfect, white teeth.

"Fix me some grub please, baby." His smile matched hers, his hand caressing her rear end while she leaned towards him.

"Ok," she agreed quietly, bending to give him a peck on the lips before retreating to the safety of the kitchen.

ELEVEN

Last But Not Least

BAILEY STOOD AT THE SINK, cleaning up her mess when her uncle came in through the back door. "How is he?" the slender man demanded without preamble.

"He's good." She smiled slightly. "He's resting on the couch. What the hell happened, anyways?"

"He's inexperienced, that's what," her uncle countered. "He got his load in a bind, an' when it snapped, the rig went over with him in the driver's seat. Damn lucky he wasn't crushed."

The girl shivered at his description. "How's the gate?"

"Finished." Peter pulled off his jacket, moving into the next room. "You able to get around?" he raised his voice anxiously, taking in the lanky male sprawled across the sofa.

"Yeah, I can get around," Caleb countered, pulling himself into an upright position with pain creases etched in his rugged features. "Kathy said I'm on bed rest for forty-eight hours, though."

"All right, well you can rest as soon as we get you down to the ranch house. We're gonna hold a meeting, an' you two need to be present." He held out his hand to hoist the younger man to his feet.

Hearing her uncle's words, Bailey's gut twisted into knots. *What if they know what transpired between us?* Or had almost transpired, at any rate. *Would they be upset?* Anxious they wanted to pass judgement upon her, she inquired quietly, "Should I be worried?"

Peter stared at the girl, his jaw hanging open slightly as he considered her guilty expression. Casting the glare over to Caleb, he shrugged. "Not unless you have something to tell me that I don't know about."

The couple exchanged a hurried glance, and the young man grinned, fighting to pull on his coat. "Ignore her," he instructed. "She just figured out we're more than friends."

Her face flushed instantly at the accusation. "Hey, that's not right!"

"See?" The tall blond continued to smile. "She's off again."

A loud whoosh of air escaped her lips while she struggled with her options. Pressing her lips together firmly, she scowled, turning her attention to the dogs for the moment and making sure they would be comfortable while they were away. "Are we coming back here tonight?"

"Yeah," Pete supplied, chuckling quietly in amusement. "Soon as the meeting is over and you've had dinner, you two can come back down here with the rest of the Cross clan, if you like."

Her eyes on fire, she spat angrily, "Well, I am after all looking after the momma and her pups. Not to mention Caleb." She shoved her hands into the sleeves of her jacket forcefully. "That'd be the only reason I would need to be here and not in my own bed since I'm not actually part of the *Cross clan.*"

"Yeah, it's fine." The younger man sidled up to her, close enough to touch but resisting the temptation. "Don' get all in a huff."

"I'm not in a huff." She struggled to calm her breathing, adjusting her cap before she went outside to get into their Jeep. "You need help getting in?" she demanded outside.

"Naw, I got it." He gripped the frame for a moment while lifting a stiff leg into the passenger floorboard. Once the doors were closed, he watched her relation climb into his own vehicle and head down the road. "Have you ever had a boyfriend?" he asked quietly as she cranked the engine and allowed it to idle for a moment.

Not answering right away, she puffed warm air into her glove-covered palms, rubbing her hands together firmly while longing for a waterproof pair. Looking at him with her peripheral, she could see he stared at her straight on. Her shoulders drooping, she sighed loudly. "Only Ked," she confessed in a small voice.

"Ked," he repeated crisply. "An' how long were you an' Ked a couple?"

Turning to look him in the eye, her mouth hung wide open, aware he didn't know who she was talking about. "Only a few weeks." She swallowed visibly. "Ked's the guy you beat up. The one who attacked me."

His eyes growing wide, he ignored the ache that had begun to grow from his awkward position in the seat. "You're kidding me! That asshole is the only guy you ever dated?"

"Yes." She sniffed, blinking quickly and turning back to the wheel, ending the conversation by putting the car in reverse and backing out.

Allowing her to maneuver the vehicle in peace, Caleb's mind raced. *Oh my God. She has less relationship experience than I do!* He had always thought living in the tiny community had put him at a disadvantage in that department. While they passed slowly in front of the greenhouse, he asked in a hushed tone, "Why didn't you ever date anyone?"

"Because my mother didn't want me to," she stated flatly, "and I always did what my mother wanted. Exactly how, without question. She wanted me to stay a virgin and go to college and get a good career started before I had anything to do with boys."

"Is that why"—he grimaced—"why you've never been with anyone?"

Blinking back more drops of sadness, she demanded loudly, "Do we really have to talk about this?" They had pulled up behind the other vehicles, and she threw the shifter into park.

"Well, we don' have t' talk about it right this second, but eventually, we're gonna need t' clear the air about this."

She sighed loudly. "Ok, have your say. What's wrong with you being my first boyfriend?"

"I thought Ked was your first," he corrected.

"He doesn't count." Her voice grew loud. "I only dated him because I thought it would piss my uncle off…and he would send me home." Her confession took the wind out of her sails, and she felt defeated. "You're the only guy I've ever been interested in." Her eyes slanted over to take in his features in the dim light of the setting sun. "There were always boys who asked but no one I wanted to be with."

"I won' be your secret lover," he stated calmly. "If you wanna be my girl, you need t' be willing t' go public."

Her tongue giving off an odd clicking noise of disgust, Bailey could feel the knot of terror in her gut. "You mean you want everyone to know we're together?"

"Yeah," he replied almost before she finished speaking. "If you're ready for us t' be bumpin' uglies, you're ready t' hold my hand in front of other people. Otherwise, there won't be none o' that goin' on!"

"Fine!" she blew up, wafting her hand towards the windows, where a few faces peered out at them. "Then I'm glad we didn't get too carried away today," she spat angrily, exiting the vehicle and leaving him to figure out how he was going to get inside.

Stomping through the front door, the girl pulled off her hat and gloves, eager to make a plate. *And sit with my brothers.* The thought had formed before she could stop it, and a fresh wave of tears filled her eyes. Unwilling to wipe them away, she turned and headed up the stairs, making it into their room and taking a seat on the lower bunk.

Allowing her drops of sadness to coat her cheeks, Bailey crossed her arms and rocked back and forth for several minutes before she realized a male form watched her from the shadows of the hall. "What are you doing?" she demanded loudly.

"Are you not gonna eat?" Caleb asked softly, moving more into the light and leaning against the frame.

"I'm not really hungry."

Daring to move further in, he nodded. "Yeah, me neither."

Instantly, her eyes shot up to glare at him. "Yes you are! You need to eat to keep up your strength so you can get better!"

Chuckling quietly, Caleb took a seat on the mattress next to her. "You're funny, you know that?"

Ignoring the jab, she looked away. "I'd really like to be alone right now."

Raising his right hand, he traced her hairline with his fingers, pushing the long strands behind her ear. "Don't be scared, baby. I'm not gonna hurt you."

Her lips puckered at his term of endearment. "My family was never close, Caleb," she confessed. "We never gave hugs or shared time together. I don't know that I ever even saw my parents kiss one another," she continued, cutting her eyes over at him. "I'm not sure if I can be who you want me to be. I'm tired of being what everyone else wants."

"What do you want?"

She blinked at him, her mind turning how he made her feel—how he had always made her feel. "I liked being best friends." She sighed. "I've never had that. I'm scared if things change, you really won't be anymore."

"I'll always be your best friend, little bit." His white teeth flashed. "If things move t' the next step, it jus' means more. Not less."

"Are you sure?" she caught his hand, entwining his fingers with her own. "And what are all your friends and family going to think? About us..." Her voice quavered at the uncertainty. "You know they don't like me."

"Bailey, they already know," he stated flatly. He stared at her, waiting for her response until he realized she didn't have one. "Baby, everyone sees the way we are together. Yeah, we're best friends. But we've been somethin' more for months now. Even before we went back t' Midland."

"No, we haven't," she gasped, wanting desperately to deny she could be that transparent. Realizing she had been toying with the idea for months, she sighed loudly. "Ok, you're right. But it scares me. I'm not used to allowing people to get close to me, especially in public," she confessed.

He laughed again, standing and pulling her up with him. "It's ok, little bit. We'll take it slow, ok? Everyone else may be used t' the idea, but I think you need time to adjust."

Squeezing his hand, she blinked up at him. "So what do I do?"

"Jus' act naturally." He traced her jaw with his free digits. "An' stop gettin' all booty hurt when someone points it out. If you feel like you need to deny somethin', take a deep breath. You're not foolin' anyone when you do. Except yourself." He grinned again, dropping his mouth to taste her briefly. "We need t' get downstairs," he said softly, "so we can find out what this meeting's about."

Retaining his hold on her, he led her to the stairs, where they descended side by side. Arriving at the bottom, she surveyed the group, all of the adults having taken seats around the living room while the remainder of the children cleaned up the kitchen and stayed out of sight. Her palm growing sweaty pressed against his, Bailey resisted the urge to tear her digits away. *Breathe,* she commanded. *Don't deny.*

"Well, now that everyone's accounted for," their matriarch began, "I guess it's time we discussed how we're gonna handle this situation."

Bailey stiffened, and Caleb gave her a squeeze.

"As you all know, some o' our family 're still trapped over in Pouty. An' some o' our family's been killt by those bastards!" her voice grew loud. "An' I, for one, ain' gonna stand for it!"

"Easy, Mom." John Cross got to his feet. "No one here's denyin' that we gotta get our people back. But there's a smart way t' go about this, an' startin' a war with our closest neighbors ain't a good way t' go about it."

"They started the war," Peter piped up. "Tasing us and taking all our supplies was bad enough, but they killed some of our men. That's unforgivable."

"Well, then, we need t' be crafty," the other man allowed. "T' be honest, I's surprised they didn't show up over here today, after what took place last night."

Bailey twitched at the comment, and Caleb released her hand, opting to put his arm around her instead, while he pointed out quietly, "No one's actually said what you did to them." He drew a deep breath, wincing at the sharp stab of pain the action produced. "Well?"

The two older men exchanged a glance. "We got out," Pete clarified. "Some of them were killed in the process. And we burned one of their buildings—their jail house," he concluded while staring at the floor in front of him.

"Oh, shit!" Bailey could feel her gut tighten. "And you didn't think they might hurt those who hadn't gotten away in retaliation?"

"No," Luis countered. "We have one of theirs." He indicated the young woman who had been quietly sitting to his left on the leather sofa. "An' we've taken back quite a bit of our supplies."

"An' their helicopter," Devon chimed in with pride at his part.

"Yeah, an' that," Luis continued. "They'll want to make a trade."

"And what if they don't want to make a trade?" the girl demanded forcefully, stepping out of Caleb's grasp and moving into the center of the room. "It's my brothers' lives you're toying with, and I don't like it!"

Seeing the glares from the older members of the community, the girl drew herself up to her full height, ready to make a stand. "Look, you guys never have given me a fair shake around here! I know I'm not the one you wanted, and you would just as soon I had been taken care of and was gone already." She paused, seeing a few of them look away. "Yeah, I know all about that shit!"

Cutting an icy glare over at Luis, she continued, "You shouldn't have left them! They are the youngest members here and the least able to look out for themselves. It wasn't right, and you know it!"

"Bailey," her uncle soothed, "we didn't have a choice. We couldn't locate them, and we had to get out of there while we could."

"What do you mean you couldn't locate them?" Her eyes darted around the group accusingly. "You don't know where they are?"

"Tha's right," Devon agreed. "We got no idea where they took 'em. An' we had to git, but we won' leave 'em there. We have this meetin' so we can decide how we're gonna get 'em back."

Bailey stared at his large brown eyes, noticing the way his new wife held onto his hand firmly. "Ok, what do you have in mind?"

"First, we get situated here," Michael intervened. "We got the gate up, and that's the main thing. Then, we can send someone over to act as our representative, negotiate for their return."

"And who the hell would take on such a task?" she demanded incredulously.

A lengthy silence followed, each of them casting eyes around the group, waiting for one of them to volunteer. When no one appeared eager to take on the job, Connie spoke up. "I'll go."

Peter stared at their oldest female, wanting to choose his words carefully. "Mom, that's a hell of an offer, an' we all appreciate your sacrifice," he began, "but you're not a negotiator."

The elderly woman gave him a toothy grin. "Don' like what I have t' say, now do ya? Well tha's tough! I'm the one that means the least aroun' here. Old I am, an' not got many years left as it is. If they kill me, we ain' lost much."

Bailey audibly gasped. "You would do that for them, knowing you might not come back?"

"Oh, child"—she shook her head at the girl—"I ain' doin' it for them. It'd be for all o' us. So you can go on an' have your future. Besides, if my negotiations don' go well, then it gets nasty. I know there's more o' them than us, but if they cain't leave us alone, they don' leave us much choice."

"I could talk to them," Bonny spoke up, her green eyes wide with fear. "Maybe they'll listen to me." When no one responded, she stood, walking slowly to the door and lifting her coat off of the rack. After she exited, an audible gasp filled the room, as if several had been holding their breaths.

"I'll take her with me," Connie announced. "I'll give her back t' them as a peace offerin'. One hostage don' do us much good anyways, an' maybe it'll buy us some time."

"Then I'll go, too," Luis volunteered, "if you'll let me." No one responded to his offer. He leaned back into the couch, his arms across his chest. "Or not."

"When you goin'?" John demanded, having held his tongue long enough. "My wife's among the missin', an' I'd sure like t' have her back."

"A few days, John." The old woman nodded. "Get us situated, an' I'll go in three days." Leaving it at that, she returned to her chores, allowing the rest of the group to go about their business.

Glancing over at Caleb, Bailey could tell he was tired and probably in pain. Following Connie into the kitchen, she inquired, "Would there be any chance Caleb and I could take our dinner back to the house? I think he needs to rest now."

Without a sound, Connie's hands began to prepare two plates, covering them and offering them to the girl. When Bailey reached to take them, her wrinkled lips spoke in a hushed voice, "You take care o' that boy."

"Yes, ma'am, I intend to." Bailey grinned shyly.

"No," she tried again, "I ain' talkin' 'bout right now. He's picked you. Why, I don' know. There's much better choices 'mong the girls that was raised here. Still, he's laid his stock in you."

Bailey glared at her sharp blue orbs, holding her denial in check. After a long moment, she swallowed and agreed, "I will do my best to deserve him."

"Good. I will do my best t' git yur brothers back." Turning her back on her, she dismissed the girl.

Exiting the kitchen, she found Caleb seated on the bottom few steps, looking more beaten than ever. Arriving with their dinner in hand, she used a quiet tone, "Do you need help getting into the car?"

"No." He grimaced, getting to his feet. "I can make it." His eyes dropping to their portions, he nodded. "Thanks. I really am looking forward to getting home."

His gaze unconsciously flittered over to her uncle, and the girl wondered what they had been discussing while she was in the kitchen retrieving the meal. Deciding to let it go, she put down the items long enough to get her jacket on, as well as help Caleb into his. Then retrieving the food, the couple said their goodnights and headed out the door.

TWELVE

Girl Talk

ARRIVING BACK at the Cross house, Bailey exited the vehicle and retrieved their plates from the back seat. Inside, she kicked on the oven and placed them inside to warm while Caleb sank down into one of the straight-back chairs with a loud moan. "Oh my God, that feels good."

A wall at his back, the nest of pups lay to his left, where the proud momma had jumped up to greet him affectionately. Giving her a few strokes, he grinned. "I think she's really taken t' bein' here. An' I think she needs a trip outdoors."

Letting Patches out to do her business, the girl kneeled down next to the pups wrapped in the blanket, adjusting them inside their bed. Retrieving one, she held it up so that he could reach it easier, commenting quietly, "So, when do we give them names?"

"Oh." He gave the small canine a once over while holding it suspended in front of him. "I think they're gonna be all right. You can name 'em if you want."

"I've never had a pet before," she reminded him with a wry grin. "I have no idea what we should call them."

"Well, we can wait an' see what their personalities turn out like."

Bailey replaced the pup he had been inspecting next to the others and let their mother back inside. Putting their dinner on the table, she sat beside him with a small grin. "Did I do better tonight?"

"Do better?"

"During the meeting, I let you put your arm around me." She shifted her eyes over at him anxiously, hoping that he had been pleased.

"Yeah." He nodded. "That was a start. When you can do that an' it's not an effort or sumthin' you gotta think about, we'll be ready for th' next step."

At that, the back door opened, and Carson came bounding in. "Hey guys!"

"Hey, Cars," Caleb shot back. "Where's Dad?"

"He's comin'." The boy shook out his red hair and hung up his outer wear. "Glad I get to be home tonight," he tossed over his shoulder as he dashed out of the room.

Entering a few minutes later, John frowned at the couple. Pulling off his own winter protection, he commanded, "Make some coffee, girl."

Bailey froze in mid bite, cutting her eyes over at Caleb and whispering loudly, "Is he serious?" The slap to the side of her head came without warning, and she dropped the fork with a sharp yelp. "What the hell did you do that for?" A searing pain shot through her ear as she spoke, and she covered her cartilage, her fingers detecting the warmth of the wounded flesh.

Taking an empty seat, the older man glared across the table at his son, daring him to protest. "My house, my rules. Make me some damn coffee!"

Sliding the chair back, Bailey rubbed the bruised spot on her head, pulling out the pot and glaring at the back of his while she filled it, momentarily wishing she could use the vessel to return the blow.

The machine set, she tentatively reclaimed her chair at the table, where Caleb continued to eat as if nothing had happened.

Staring at her plate for a moment, the girl's appetite had vanished, so she excused herself and made her way to the bathroom wearing a small pout.

As soon as the door closed, John began to laugh. "Nice to see you gettin' a handle on things, son." He pointed in her direction with a thumb. "Jus' try t' keep it down tonight."

"We're not sleepin' together," Caleb informed him coolly.

"You's in bed with 'er this mornin'." John grinned. "'Course I think you shoulda waited 'til you's married, but I know how kids are these days."

Running his fingers through his blond spikes, he grimaced. "If I wasn't hurt, we wouldn't be havin' this conversation."

"Wha's that supposed t' mean?" The older man's expression darkened.

"You ever touch her again, an' you will find out." Caleb pushed back his empty plate and glared at the man across from him. "She ain't Mom, an' she don' belong t' you. You got no business layin' a hand on 'er. Don't do it again." Standing, he allowed his threat to fall flat across the table and worked his way to the bathroom, where he knocked lightly on the door. "Bailey, you ok in there?"

"Yes," her voice came from the other side. "I'll be out in a few minutes."

He could hear the water begin to run and turned to the living room to help get their sleeping arrangements lined out. Ignoring his father, who ambled up the stairs, Caleb moved back to the kitchen, scraping the remnants into the bowl for the dog before washing the plates.

"I would have done that." She startled him when she spoke.

"It's ok. I'm not totally helpless." He grinned, stacking the items to return to the ranch house on their next trip. "I'm sorry he acted that way. He won't do it again."

"Does he beat your mom?" she asked in a shaky voice.

Giving his left shoulder a shrug, he looked at her squarely. "Not like he used to. I guess she learned how to keep him happy, an' he don' lay into her so much anymore."

Blinking slowly, she glared at him through her swollen eyes. He could see she had been crying, the bright red ear poking out through the hair she used in an attempt to cover it. "That's why Uncle Pete always thinks you're going to hurt me. Because of your dad."

Leaning on the counter, Caleb could feel the warm flush of shame rising from his chest. "I need to lie down," he made the excuse.

Her hands firm, she grasped him and allowed him to lean on her while she guided him to the couch, where he caught her fingers and held her there once he was seated. "I would never raise a hand to you, little bit. I want you t' know that. An' he won't ever touch you again. If he does, you let me know, an' I'll take care of it."

Giving his digits a small shake, she sighed loudly. "Are you sleeping on the couch?"

"Yeah." He wafted his free hand at the mattress. "You stay down there, an' I'll leave you alone." Tugging on her appendage gently, he grinned up at her, and she slid onto his lap, as she had before.

Leaning her forehead against his, she emitted a small sigh. "Everything has been so up and down. I feel exhausted."

"I know, baby." He massaged her back, lifting his face and planting a small, deliberate kiss on her lips. "Get some rest, an' I'll see you in th' mornin'."

Climbing off of him, Bailey obeyed, removing her boots and stretching out across the makeshift bed. Covering herself with the blankets and closing her lids firmly, she listened to him breathe in the darkness until she fell asleep. Waking to bright light and the sound of voices the following morning, she laid her forearm over her eyes for a moment before summoning the strength to get up.

Her fingers finding her freshly wounded anatomy, she could tell it still felt swollen but hoped at least the color had waned. Making her way into the bathroom, she changed clothes and prepared to face the day, her uncertainty about the future reigning supreme.

Upon exiting, she discovered the mattress no longer lay in the living room floor. Scowling at the empty space, she heard John laugh, so she cut the angry look over to him. "What's going on?"

"I tol' you, my house, my rules. You can either get in bed with Caleb an' be a good wife, or you can go home." He wafted a hand towards the ranch house over the sink where he stood. "Either way makes no nevermind t' me." Turning his back on her, he pulled on his coat and gloves. "Breakfast is down the road. Carson!" he hollered loudly. "Le's go boy! We got snow t' shovel."

"Down the road!" She pulled her hands to her hips, watching the door close behind him. "You have no business traipsing back and forth just to eat," she informed Caleb firmly.

"Well, then I guess we pack up and move to the ranch house, or you can go an' bring me back some food. But I definitely think you need t' take the dogs an' get outta here," his voice sounded listless.

"Why? What's wrong with the dogs?"

Holding up a hand, he leaned against the chair in front of him. "Trust me. My ol' man's a stubborn son of a bitch, an' he don' really like you. Or women in general, I guess I should say. It'd be better if you didn' stay here anymore."

"Then I'll pack your things and take you with me," she stated firmly. "I have no idea how we're going to work it out, but there's a couch there and the boys' bunk beds to boot. And he doesn't like the dog? I think your dad's an asshole, Caleb!"

"He is not," Carson defended from the doorway, anger coloring his face.

"Carson!" she clipped in shock. "I'm so sorry. I thought you were outside with your father!"

"Obviously not," he quipped, pointing his finger at her while addressing Caleb. "I tol' you we shoulda got rid o' her. Now she's splittin' us up an' turnin' you against us!"

"No, she's not." The older boy shook his head. "You don't understand. That's all. Go help Dad before he comes back in here lookin' for you. An' don't worry about us. It's time for me t' make my own way, Cars. That's all."

Glaring at the girl as he passed by, the boy covered his red shocks of hair with a stocking cap and pulled on his coat and gloves. Exiting with a loud slam of the door, his opinion of the situation remained glaringly obvious.

"I'll help you pack my stuff." Caleb grimaced at the girl.

"No, you sit and rest," she commanded, angry that she was having to move the people from the house who needed to stay put most. "I'll pack a nice bag for you and load the Jeep. You want coffee while you wait?" She eyed the empty pot.

"Sure, baby." He smiled, taking a seat in the chair closest to the pups so he could mess with them. "You're such a kind-hearted person," he commented when she placed his cup before him. "I'm not sure I deserve you."

She tousled his hair, grinning from ear to ear. "Well, you don't have me yet," she teased, dropping her face next to his before she kissed him. After a brief exchange of moist tongues, she giggled. "But I'm beginning to really like the idea of it." Standing up straight, her long tresses bounced as she mounted the stairs and headed to his room to retrieve his essentials.

Arriving at their destination a short while later, Bailey helped the injured man into the kitchen, where she put him at the table and served him a plate. "Where can we put the dogs?" she asked Connie point blank.

Stopping in mid motion, the older woman turned from her sink of dishes. "What dogs?"

"The one the Smalls had, I think," she explained. "I'm not really sure. Caleb and I found her after we got here, and she had three puppies. Preferably here in the kitchen, so they can be warm and she can get in and out easy, but wherever you say is fine."

Continuing with her chore, Connie chuckled. "Decided to move back down here?"

"Yes," Bailey spat, taking the exit to retrieve the animals. Returning shortly, she placed the blanket in the corner, opposite the back door and behind the table. "There we go." She patted the dog generously while her stomach emitted a loud growl. Standing, she then moved to make her plate from what remained of the food. "I guess I should have gotten here sooner. Can we save the scraps for the dog?"

"I suppose we can." Her wrinkled lips pursed for a moment. "Is that boy stayin' here with you?" she spoke of Caleb as if he weren't even present.

"Yes, ma'am," he chimed in. "I'd like t' take one o' the bunks in the boys' room, until they return, if that would be ok."

"That'd be fine." The matriarch finished the dishes and allowed the pair to eat. When they had finished, she laid down her own rules. "You won' be sleepin' together in my house, you got that? Sex is for married couples. I think it's disgraceful, what that girl done!" her reference unmistakable.

"Yes, ma'am," Bailey agreed, exhaling a sigh of relief when the other woman left the room. Dropping her voice, she whispered, "She really is remarkable."

"She's one of a kind," the blond agreed, getting to his feet. "I'm gonna go lay down, little bit."

Rising, the girl followed, hauling his bag up the stairs for him and placing it in the room where he would sleep. Closing the door behind her when she left, she allowed him to stretch out on the bottom bunk to get some rest. Hearing the faint sound of a baby crying up the stairs, she moved towards her own floor to investigate.

Discovering the tall blonde in the room that Devon had shared with Nung, she knocked lightly on the frame. "Hi."

"Hey." The other girl looked over her shoulder. "What a surprise!"

"Not really," Bailey countered evenly. "Caleb and I are moving down here. His father is a real jerk."

"Showed you his true colors, did he?" Amanda flicked her hair, lifting the infant from her tiny makeshift crib. "I hope you don' mind. It's time t' feed."

"No, not at all." Bailey eagerly perched on one of the beds, watching as the new mother bared a breast and eased down into the rocking chair, placing the tiny mouth against her nipple.

Tossing a blanket over herself once she had settled in, she smiled. "So, you an' Caleb are official then."

"Oh my God. I'm sorry." The girl instantly threw up her hands in surrender. "I didn't even think about—"

"Hey, don' worry," Amanda cut her off with a laugh. "We was over a long time ago, even if it was hard fur me t' admit. 'Sides, Dev loves me real good." Moving the covering so she could see her baby's eyes staring up at her, "An' I'm glad my little lapse in judgement didn' ruin things for you."

"No, it didn't." Bailey suddenly felt awkward sharing girl talk with Caleb's ex-lover. "Maybe I should go."

Making a quick exit, she moved down the hall to her own room, where she set about returning her things to their proper places. Skipping down the stairs, she retrieved her trash bag of gear from the car. It being from their last trip from Midland, it held all of her winter clothes, and she put those items away as well.

Stretching out across the bed when she was done, she lay still, listening to the familiar creak of the windmill outside. A small smile teasing her lips, she relaxed into the comfort of the sound and drifted off to sleep.

THIRTEEN

So It Is

WHAT CONNIE HAD ESTIMATED WOULD BE three days, turned out to be two weeks, although it wasn't exactly her choice in the matter. The morning following the meeting, the entire group had awoken to discover another snowstorm had taken place in the darkness, adding at least six inches to the icy mixture that coated the ground.

Using the backhoe, one of the men cleared all the streets, and most of the men and some of the women pitched in to clear the paths to each of the houses. It proved to be a futile effort, as the temperature remained below freezing, and more continued to fall in long spurts. After seven days, Caleb had sufficiently healed enough, and he ventured outside to have a look around, wishing he could help. However, in the end, he remained delegated to dog duty.

Calling another meeting at the two-week marker, what remained of the *menfolk* met in private, having some hard decisions to make. When they came out, Connie and the girl from Pouty were bundled up and given a Jeep. It had further been decided that Luis would do the driving, which he eagerly accepted. Two of the vehicles that they had taken from the other town had been equipped with snow chains, and one of these was sacrificed for the trip.

Bailey held Caleb's hand under the canopy next to the stables while they watched the group exit through the gate. Glancing across at the large empty space that had once been the arena, sadness crept over her and she sighed. "I don't think they're coming back."

"Don't say that." He gave her a squeeze. "We have t' stay positive, little bit."

"I know," she agreed. "But it's so hard. And I'm going to miss that old lady, I think."

"We all are," Caleb chuckled, tugging on her digits. "Come on. I'm supposed t' go check in with Kathy today."

Walking through the path created by the cleared road, the couple arrived on the other side of the compound several minutes later. Entering the med center, Caleb eagerly climbed onto the table, a little less gingerly than he had the last time he had been there.

"Well, you seem to be getting around better," the nurse observed, pulling out her stethoscope to give him a listen.

"Yeah." The young man grinned. "I'm still sore, but at least it don' hurt t' breathe anymore." Standing, he removed his clothes for her, so she could have a better look.

After a thorough examination, she removed the brown bandages from his chest to investigate further. "I'm not going to X-ray you yet. I think you're coming along nicely. I want to leave you unwrapped as well, but don't overdo it. No shoveling snow!" she commanded, causing the couple to laugh loudly.

"Anything I *can* do?" he asked while putting his clothes on.

"You can observe." Her eyes darted over at the girl for an instant. "And while you're both here, I'd like to have a little talk with you about birth control."

"Oh my God!" Bailey exclaimed loudly. "Why does EVERYONE assume that we're sleeping together!"

Taken by surprise, the older woman held up her hands. "Whoa,

whoa, I'm only trying to be helpful. No offense intended. I'm the medical expert, and I wish that people would keep that in mind and stop taking things into their own hands around here."

Bailey stared at her, the wheels turning. "Is someone else pregnant?"

Her jaw dropped, Kathy took a step back. "It would be unprofessional of me to discuss anyone else with you."

Shooting Caleb a half-grin, the girl knew she was on to something. "Well, don't worry. We're not physically involved, so there won't be any surprises coming from us."

"Well, just the same, I'd like for you to be prepared." Kathy opened a drawer, removing a box of prophylactics and handing them to the man next to her.

"Uh, thanks." He accepted the small box, giving it a frown. "But really, by the time we're ready for these, we won' have t' worry about gettin' into trouble." When the woman failed to take them back, he placed them on the small table next to the bed, giving the container a tiny wave. "You ready, little bit?"

"Yes," the girl answered, still in shock. Turning to the door, she exited without looking back. Pausing her step enough for him to catch her in front of the gym, she laughed loudly. "Can you believe that? And someone else here is pregnant! I knew it was going to happen. I knew it!"

"Keep your voice down," he instructed, reaching for her hand.

"Ok," she agreed in a much lower tone. "But I was right!"

"Yeah, but that don' mean much. It's really not a good thing in the end. Can't wait to see what the *menfolk* do about it."

Arriving back at the ranch house a short time later, they discovered the house had fallen into an uproar. Seeing Peter rushing around the living room, apparently packing random items, Bailey demanded loudly, "What the hell's going on?"

"We're moving to Lawson," he stated flatly, while trying to appear calm.

"What?" Caleb interrupted. "I thought that was bad for morale."

"It is," Pete admitted, stepping closer to them so he could lower his voice, "but with the Pouty girl outta here, that gives us more options."

"You were staying up top so she wouldn't find out about the cave?" Bailey speculated.

"Partly, yes." Her uncle nodded. "But maintaining the heat in so many dwellings is becoming more difficult. Two of the turbines are down, an' we may lose a third. Keeping the underground chamber warm is practically energy free since it stays at a higher temperature naturally. Plus, we'll be safer, no matter what comes at us. Go pack your stuff, Bailey-girl. Caleb an' I need to have a talk."

"Oh God." She rolled her eyes, almost certain she knew what the topic was going to be. Giving her best friend a knowing smirk, she stomped up the stairs to comply.

Caleb watched her slender frame disappear around the turn before he met the other man's stare. "Ok, what?"

"You need to make a choice," the older man put it bluntly. "You know as well as I do, quarters are going to be tight down below. I'm going to give Bailey the bed that was meant for me an' Brenda, an' I'll take one of the bunks in the other room. I want you to share it with her."

"I have a bed, remember?" Caleb shook his head. "I doubt my ol' man is still mad. Besides, I'm not gonna pressure her t' do it. I told her she needed time, an' I'm gonna give it t' her." His gaze returned to the stairs, his mind back on the young woman on the third floor.

"Caleb, you're a good man." A hand clamped onto his shoulder while he was being praised. "But you have to listen to me. There are only three of the *menfolk* left, an' things are gonna come to a head. Your father would like to run this place all on his own, an' Mike would go along with that, I'm fairly certain."

"So what're you sayin'?"

"I'm sayin' the two of you need to consummate your relationship."

"What!" the younger man exclaimed loudly, taking a step back to remove the other man's appendage from his own. "First off, no one even talks like that anymore. An' second off, I'm not gonna force her!"

"You don't have to force her. In fact, I would prefer that you didn't. But..." He paused, glancing around to make sure the conversation was still private. "Everyone needs to be clear that you two are involved."

"An' why is that?" Caleb demanded, his anger beginning to boil. "This wouldn' have anything t' do with someone else comin' up pregnant around here, would it?"

The color drained from the older man's face. "What do you know about that?"

"Nothing," he shot back, running his fingers through his hair in an agitated state. "I don' know a damned thing."

Taking the stairs in twos, at least for the first flight, Caleb made his way to the third floor and stomped to the end of the hall. Entering her room unannounced, he closed the door loudly behind him. "Your uncle wants me to fuck you."

Spinning around from her packing, Bailey only stared with her mouth hanging open. After a long silence, she regained her voice. "Are you sure?"

"Yup. Pretty sure. He said we need to *consummate* our relationship."

"Wow, that's blunt! And a bit pushy on top of that."

"Yeah, an' it scares the shit outta me, if you wanna know the truth. Somethin's goin' on, an' he don' wanna tell us what."

"So, he wants us to sleep together, or to get married, or what?"

"He didn' specify. That's exactly what he said, an' I'm so pissed right now I wanna kick th' shit outta someone!"

Her face shifted from surprise to horror. "You don't really want me, do you?" she concluded in a dejected tone.

"Don't really want you... What?" He wrinkled his brow. "How could you say that?" He opened his palm to the ceiling, shoving the hand towards her. "O' course I want you. I've wanted you since th' first time I ever saw you, back in Illinois." The words were out before he could stop them, his skin growing paler after their utterance. "Shit. I didn' mean it like that, Bailey!"

Scrunching her nose, she retorted, "Well, I think we should just do it an' get it over with."

He gaped at her. "Whadda you mean get it over with? What happened to it bein' perfect?" His hands shot to his hips as he rebuked her.

"It isn't going to be perfect." She sniffed loudly. "Everything is messed up and ruined, no matter how you slice it. The world is crashed. There isn't even a connection to the internet anymore! It's gone, Caleb! All gone! So, if you want to fuck me and get it over with, then that's fine by me. At least I won't have to worry about it anymore, and it'll be done."

Staring at her, he couldn't believe his ears. "When did the internet disappear?"

"A few days ago. I've been logging in once a day to see if anything has changed, and it's only been getting worse. Then it was all gone—no connection." A tear spilled over and rolled down her cheek. "It's over, Caleb. The world as we know it is *gone*." She broke down into loud sobs.

Stepping towards her, he wrapped her in his arms, thankful he could do so. "Shhshh." Running a firm hand down her back, he nuzzled her scalp through her auburn waves. "Easy, baby. You don' really wanna do that. Not like this."

"Yes, I do." She grasped at his shirt, pressing herself against him. "I don't want to think about it anymore. I don't want it to be an issue anymore. If it's not with you, now, then who will it be?" she whined. "One of the men from Pouty, when they force themselves on me?"

"Don't say that." He tightened his grip. "They ain' gonna get the better o' us or force you t' do anything!"

"You don't know that." She pulled herself away, wiping angrily at her tears. "You don't know anything, Caleb, any more than the rest of us do. They have us outnumbered, and who knows what all tricks they have up their sleeves!" Her tone grew softer. "Please, Caleb. Please don't make me beg."

His blue eyes stared at her, finding it hard to focus. Rocking his jaw side to side, he considered her plea and her uncle's possible motives for pushing the issue. *You knew eventually it would come to this,* he reminded himself with a loud sigh. *Quit being afraid, an' do what you gotta do.*

"Take your clothes off," he instructed quietly, unbuttoning his shirt. Turning his back so that he didn't have to watch her in the fading light, he continued to remove his clothing until all that remained was his cotton briefs. Looking over his shoulder at that point, he could see that she had complied but had stopped at her undergarments as well and stood staring at him. "Well?"

Her bottom lip trembling, she clasped her hands in front of her, and stammered, "I wanted it to be perfect," she confessed, followed by a loud broken sob.

"Well, ours wasn't," he stated gruffly, taking ahold of her arm and removing her bra before pushing her back onto the bed. Grasping her panties, she gave no resistance when he removed them. Pulling his own covering out of the way, he lay over her, staring into her clear green eyes for a long moment. "I really am sorry," he allowed more softly, before he roughly put an end to their dilemma.

FOURTEEN

White Wedding

BAILEY AWOKE to the sound of the windmill squealing outside. The noise brought her a small amount of comfort, indicating she remained inside the ranch house, at least for the time being. Shifting to stretch, she made two discoveries: she was naked, and she was not alone.

Stifling her urge to scream, the events of the evening before flooded into her fragmented thoughts. "Oh God!"

Hearing her utterance, Caleb rolled over, parting her legs and pushing his nakedness against her.

"What are you doing?" she gasped.

"You're mine, remember?" He licked and bit roughly at the skin that covered the front of her neck. "Lay still, an' I won' take long."

"It was supposed to be one time, Caleb!" Her voice shrill, she pushed against his chest, as if she could remove him. An instant later, she recalled his injuries and relaxed her arms, unwilling to risk hurting him to put an end to it.

"Tha's better." He smiled against her cheek, licking her ear while his fingers weaved through her soft hair and located her scalp. His lips tracing the line of her jaw, he moaned.

"Stop that," she hissed. "Amanda will hear you! She's in the next room!"

"So what?" He gripped her tighter for a moment, breathing heavily against her hair-covered ear. When he was finished, he slid out from the covers to locate his clothing. "How do you think they made that kid o' theirs?"

"You're disgusting," she bit angrily, clutching the blanket tightly between her fingers, watching his naked form as he slowly covered it with his layers. "You're not even going to get a bath?"

"Naw. What's the point? I'm gonna fuck you again in a few hours, anyways." He tossed her a grin and exited the room.

Lifting the sheet, she glared down into the darkness, unable to make out any of her anatomy. "I feel so tingly," she whispered to herself with a violent shudder. Climbing out of bed, she realized she would have to get dressed to get to the bathroom for her shower, so she donned her previously worn clothing to accomplish the task, carrying fresh attire under her arm.

Once she had washed away the evidence of their encounter, Bailey dressed in her usual cold-weather items, faintly aware that the tingle she had experienced earlier that morning persisted. Brushing out her long, auburn locks, she pulled them up into a ponytail and flicked it a few times in the playful mood that had settled over her. Exiting the small room, she returned to her quarters and made quick work of the rest of her packing before she went downstairs.

Arriving on the ground floor, she discovered that everyone in town had gathered in the house for breakfast. Pasting on her best smile, she refused to have her discomfort made public and sauntered into the kitchen with her head held high. Catching sight of Caleb leaning against the counter, her heart leapt into overdrive, beating wildly against her ribs. *His hair is wet. He did have a shower!*

Waiting for her to come to him, the young man glared at her while she ambled about the small space, gathering her morning meal. When she finally moved within reach, he shifted to clasp her hand and pulled her closer to him, returning his rear end to the edge of the counter, her body pressed full length against his.

Dropping her plate on the flat surface behind him, the urge to play along washed over her, and she pushed her face up to his. Their lips meeting gently at first, the kiss quickly deepened into much more, bringing a hot flush of embarrassment to her round cheeks when she realized all conversation had ceased and everyone stared. Giggling quietly, she retrieved her platter and left him standing there while she moved to the dining room to consume her meal.

Watching her rear end sway as she disappeared through the door frame, Caleb broke into a wide grin, giving her uncle a wink. Lifting his mug of warm brew, the older man repaid the gesture with a small nod and moved to the larger room in the front of the house, calling loudly, "Everyone here now?"

"I believe so," John replied from the sofa, rubbing his hands together eagerly. Producing a large sheet of paper, he spread it on the coffee table before him. "Everyone should be packed and ready to go. Once we move into the caves, no one will be allowed on the surface except on official business. The more we come an' go, the greater our chances o' being discovered, so we gotta be discreet."

"Agreed." Pete, raised his cup in a mock salute, shifting his gaze over at the third remaining *menfolk*. "What say you, Mike?"

"Agreed." The other man pursed his lips. "But we need to rearrange some of the sleeping quarters, since some of our situations have changed."

"I got that handled." John wafted a hand towards the map that lay before him. "Since the Foxes no longer need their quarters, I'm putting Devon an' 'Manda in that room. An' since my boy has taken up with the Dewitt girl, they'll be in the Mason master bedroom, at Pete's request." He shot the other man a quick glance. "Or have you changed your mind?"

"Naw. It's theirs. I'll take a bunk bed in the other room, an' when the boys get back, we'll square that away." He grinned. "What else?"

"Well, 'Manda's move left Jennifer alone in one o' the Knight rooms, an' since Allen was killed, Don has come to me an' asked for her hand." He glared at Paula while he spoke, curious if she were aware of the arrangement.

Shooting up from her perch on the edge of a chair, the girl's mother shrieked, "You can't be serious! Jen is barely eighteen, and that man is over thirty! You already forced one of my girls to marry one of them. Surely you don't intend to take both..."

"Well, we don' got a lot o' options here, now do we? He's asked, an' I gave my permission." He cut the woman an icy glare, daring her to challenge his authority. "There'll be a weddin' soon enough, an' I expect my boy'll be announcing their intent as well."

Caleb stiffened, having heard Bailey's gasp from the other room. Moving to peek at her through the door frame, he grinned, giving her a small wave of his hand to quiet her while his father continued.

"Lastly, we've decided to post a sentry on the front gate. Twenty-four hours a day, one o' the men'll be stationed there on lookout, since the main road's the only way in, unless someone comes with another aircraft." He chopped the air with a stiff hand in the direction of the front entrance. "That means th' path between the barn an' the fence'll be cleared. Everything else'll be allowed t' fill in, an' we go into hidin'."

Bailey's face shot up from her meal. "What about my dog?" she shrieked.

"Your dog?" John called, glaring at the girl as she entered the front room to confront him.

"Yes, she's mine." Bailey shook her ponytail in disgust. "I found her. If I hadn't, she would have died. And I've been taking care of her and her pups. Where are we going to put them?"

"Easy, little bit." Her uncle stepped forward. "We can't take them down into Lawson."

"Well, then we have to fix a place for them in one of the buildings. Over in the barn with the rest of the animals? Someone will have to come up and feed them, so taking on Patches and her puppies will not be a big deal," she insisted, putting her hands on her hips defiantly. Her eyes growing wide, she gasped, "And how are you going to get the food over to the rabbits and horses? The feed barn is on the other side of the arena."

"We're gonna stack enough over to get them by for a few weeks an' put it out a little at a time." John grinned at her, surprised she had thought of the animals at all. "Don' worry. We'll make a place for the dogs in the barn as well, an' you can take the scraps up to her. But scraps only! I don' wanna see any more o' our food bein' fed t' animals."

She stared with wide eyes, surprised he had given in. "Yes, sir." She sighed, her shoulders drooping from the mental exhaustion of the confrontation, while considering there would be a final price for it down the line.

Moving in behind her, Caleb slid his arm around her waist. "What about the greenhouse? Mom would be setting up the seed pots soon. Who's gonna take over that?"

"Well, your woman was workin' with her last summer. Let her take over until your momma gets back." John grinned at the solution, watching the way his oldest son held on to the girl protectively. "Anything else we need t' settle before we move?"

"Should I take things for the boys?" Bailey's voice came out low, the idea of not including her brothers bringing her down rapidly after her brutal win with the dogs.

"Pack them but leave them in their room. They'll be easy to fetch for them, when they get home," Peter supplied. "Anything else?"

When no one else spoke up, John stood, clearing his throat loudly. "All right, we got two hours, an' then I want everyone down an' quiet. All the women move the gear an' get set up below. Caleb, we're gonna need your help, but don't hurt yourself. You, me, an' the rest o' the men need t' meet at the barn so we can get the feed loaded an' moved." He indicated the structure that housed the feed across the parking area through the wall. "Le's go people!"

Without further delay, the entire house began to move, as if it were an ant hill that had been kicked.

Spinning in Caleb's arms, Bailey twisted to face him. "I guess this means I'll see you downstairs." Her belly flopped at the idea.

"Yeah," he agreed, leaning his forehead against hers. "You're officially with me now, little bit. You know that, right?"

A small smile tickled her lips. "Yes, I guess I am. So be careful out there, ok?"

"Sure thing, baby." He kissed the tip of her nose and followed the rest of the men outside, pulling on his coat as he went.

Watching them go, Jennifer stepped up beside the girl, who only stood an inch or so taller, and tossed her arm across her shoulder. "So, we doin' a twin weddin'?"

Bailey's eyes grew wide, staring at the girl who had never spoken to her directly. "I thought you didn't like me," she blurted.

"Meh." Jen grinned. "That was mos'ly for 'Manda's sake. I thought you's stealin' her boyfriend. But now she's got her own man, so I guess you're welcome to him."

Her brow furrowed, her green eyes sparkled. "Gee, thanks." She looked away. "Well, we can't have it outside right now anyways." She smirked coyly. "Unless you want a really white wedding."

Her laughter loud, the shorter girl punched her in the arm. "Tha's funny. See, we are gettin' along!" Walking away, she grabbed her jacket to go get her own things ready to carry below.

FIFTEEN

There Is No Peace

CONNIE FROWNED at the burned out buildings as they pulled into the compound. "I thought you said you guys burned th' jail!"

"We did." Luis's jaw hung open in disbelief.

"Oh my God." Bonny began to cry, the diner where she had worked unrecognizable. "What the hell happened?"

"I'm stumped," the man next to her faltered. "We were long gone before any of this happened, remember?"

Noticing people gathering in the street, his heart began to beat faster. Applying the brake, he brought the vehicle to a halt and slipped it into park. "I guess we get out."

"Let me go first," the girl suggested, opening the door and stepping out onto the snow. "Hey, guys!" she called loudly, giving a few of them a wave.

"What the hell are you doin' here?" Phillip Pipes practically screamed, reaching the girl first.

"They brought me home," she offered, allowing the door to close and moving away from it. "They were hoping you would let them take the rest of their people home."

Gripping her arms, he gave her a violent shake. "The rest of their people? Are you out of your God damned mind?"

"Hey!" Luis yelled, whacking the dashboard with his right fist and pointing a stiff digit at the man. "Don't do that to her!"

Staring at the man making a scene from inside the car, the leader of the community laughed, then gave the girl a good slap. "Come out here an' make me!"

Opening the door in an instant, Luis bolted out, clearing the front of the Jeep but falling short of reaching the other man. A crowd of people grabbed him, knocking him to the ground. Kicking him repeatedly, several of the Pouty townsfolk began to chant for his head and *get a rope*, among other things.

"Oh my God! Stop!" Bonny shrieked, a pair of hands grasping her from behind and holding her in place while the mob dispensed its justice. A few minutes later, the old woman was noticed and dragged out of the back seat to join them.

"Stop this!" a loud shout could be heard over the chaos. "You stop this RIGHT NOW!"

Ignoring the voice of reason, the gathering continued to lay blows upon the man, and a few took to beating the elderly woman, sending the girl into wails of hysterics. "Please, stop! They're only here to talk!" she begged for their lives. The arm around her neck tightened, and she began to gasp. "I can't breathe." Her fingers moved desperately over the appendage in an attempt to remove it. A moment later, she lost consciousness, her body hanging limply in front of her attacker.

Bonny awoke to pitch black. Blinking into the darkness for a few minutes, she couldn't see anything, but the smell had a familiar feel. Sitting up straight, she determined she was home, in her own bed. Rising, her neck stiff, she stretched, trying to pop it to no avail. Flicking on her light, she noted she still wore the same clothes she had left The Ranch in and felt no desire to change.

Instead, she exited her chamber, finding her mother alone in the kitchen. Flopping onto a chair to watch the older woman wash dishes, she sighed loudly. "So, what happened?"

Making a loud, disgusted click with her tongue, "When do you mean? When they burned our town or when they got what they deserved?"

"Oh my God!" Bonny was on her feet. "Where's Luis, Mom? Where's Connie?" When her mother failed to respond, the girl began to cry.

"Stop that. It was damn foolish of you to run off with him," her mother's voice loud, her words were clipped. "An' even more so for you to come back!"

"Where is he, momma?" She sniffed through her tears. "Please tell me he's ok."

Pulling her hands out of the soapy water, the woman grabbed a towel to wipe them clean. Staring down at them as she did so, she exhaled slowly. "They killed him, Bonny. He's gone...and the woman. An' the two they left here the night they fled."

The squeal that followed deafening, the girl collapsed where she stood. Thrashing about, she kicked and screamed, throwing a tantrum as if she were a small child. When the flailing subsided, her mother knelt down beside her, touching her face with water-wrinkled fingers.

"I'm sorry, baby." She pursed her lips. "But I'm so glad they didn't kill you, too."

"What do you mean kill me, too?" She stared up with wide eyes, her breathing sporadic.

"Phil was holding you, choking you. If someone hadn't forced him to release you, when you passed out..." Her voice trailed away, the reality of losing her only daughter more than she could bear. "I'm so glad you're home, baby."

Slapping her hands away and rolling over, the girl got to her feet. She stumbled down the hall in agony. *Luis is gone!* Making it to the bathroom, she bellowed, gagging and spitting wads of thick saliva. When the wave of misery ebbed, she washed her face in the sink. Lifting her head, her ebony locks parted, and she stared at her green eyes in the mirror, shocked by the deep red splotches of blood that filled the whites of them. "Holy shit!"

"It's from being choked," her mother explained. "You were on the edge."

"But someone saved me," she breathed. Turning, she reached out to embrace the woman behind her. "Oh my God, Mom. I loved him! Why did they kill him?" Her wail started all over again.

"Bonny!" the command came with a firm snap. "Calm down! It's done and over, and carryin' on ain't gonna bring him back!"

Freeing her, the girl took in deep pants to calm herself. "So, what happened to all the buildings? It was like, all of them! Why are they all burned?"

"Because"—her mother patted her daughter's shoulder absently—"they set fire to one of them before they left. Only, we weren't able to put it out, an' it spread to the others. Burned 'em to the ground."

"Oh...my God." Her arm pressed to her furrowed brow, deep lines formed around her mouth. "They never meant for that to happen," she defended their actions. "They just wanted to get away!"

"And they did." The other woman shook the hair out of her face, crossing her arms while she leaned against the door frame. "So, why come back here? They had to know our people would retaliate. They have to know what's comin', for what they did!"

"They just want their people back. That's all! They don't wanna fight with us," she defended loudly. "All they want is peace an' t' be left alone!"

"There is no peace, Bonny. Not after what they've done." She blinked at her offspring for a moment. "They poisoned us. Some of the food, it was tainted, and three whole families died, children and all. They're gonna get what they deserve."

The girl stared at her, realizing what her words meant. Her mind turning, she knew tough choices lay ahead of her. "When?"

"Very soon," her mother supplied. "If they hadn't stolen our helicopter, it would'a already taken place."

"What are they going...I mean we, going to do?"

"Philip wants to crush them." The older woman stepped aside, turning her back and moving to the front room. "I say we should let them starve to death. They only got a few of their animals back, an' they can't live more than a few months on those."

Rolling her tongue inside her cheek, Bonny refused to divulge what she knew; she hadn't seen the stores or anything concrete, but she knew the people at The Ranch were not going to starve to death. "It wasn't their fault, Mom. We attacked them first. What did *Phil* expect for them to do?" Her words had grown sharp in anger at the stupidity of the situation.

"Why are you defending them?" She spun around to face her daughter squarely. "You're one of us, remember?"

"Not anymore." The girl gritted her teeth. "Not like this! You people disgust me." She lumped her parents in with the rest. "And I don' care if they kill me! They shouldn't have done it, any of it! And now there will be no peace between us." Fresh tears welled and spilled, covering her face with trails of sorrow. "We didn't want much, Mom. Why couldn't they just let us be?"

The woman stared at her daughter in bewilderment. "Go to your room, Bonny. Go to bed and get some rest. An' when you get up, I don't wanna hear you speak of that man or that woman or that place again! You're home now, an' THIS is where you belong!"

Turning her back in reserved rage, the girl stomped down the hall, slamming her bedroom door behind her. Flopping onto the bed, she allowed herself quiet tears while she brooded, her mind running in circles over what she knew. *Chris and Martha—those are the two adults who didn't get away.* Her mother had said they were dead.

But there were kids, too—two girls and two boys—who were left behind. Luis had asked her about them before they made their escape, but she had no idea where they were. *I have to find them.* She rolled over and stared at the ceiling. *I have to know if they're ok.*

Closing her eyes, she willed herself to sleep, to rest, knowing she would need her strength. *They pissed off the wrong bitch,* she whispered to herself. *I have to find the rest of them and help them get home.* She sighed heavily, her hand on her chest rising and falling in a steady pattern. *And I'll burn the rest of the God damned town to the ground if I have to, to do it!*

SIXTEEN

Pretty Reckless

BAILEY CARRIED the last load of their stuff into their tiny chamber, dropping it onto the bed. *Home, sweet home.* Her eyes swinging around the compact space once more, she emitted a small sigh. "Well, I never saw this coming," she mused aloud to herself.

Selecting a bag, she dumped the contents on top of the pile and began hanging the items in the closet, her clothes on the left and Caleb's on the right. The idea of them sharing the room gave her an odd twinge in her gut, and the memory of what they had done that morning flashed into her mind, staining her cheeks bright red.

Well, you wanted to get it over with, she admonished herself, *and it's over with.* But somehow, it hadn't occurred to her he would expect the behavior to continue, as if the first time would have been enough and things would have remained the platonic same afterwards. Emitting a small sigh, she could at least be glad that Caleb had been her first and not Ked. *I wonder whatever happened to him, anyways.*

Of course, she never saw him after they returned to Midland, not even at the high school. Therefore, she could only assume that his family had moved to the other school's district or left town. *With the way people came and went, there's really no telling.*

Tackling another bag, she made quick work of the chore and moved on to making the bed. Only a full-sized, like the one she had in the ranch house, she smiled at how Caleb's feet would hang off the end, since hers almost did. Smiling to herself, she finished straightening and moved out into the front part of their tiny apartment to put that in order.

Lastly, she tackled her uncle's clothing, placing it in the small closet that had been meant for her brothers. Making up the bottom bunk for the man as well, a sadness settled over her, causing tears to drip onto the sheets while she smoothed them. Her hands slowed, it took her longer to complete the task, and her two hours were up by the time she finished.

"Hey!" Deanna called to the girl from the outer doorway. "Get movin'! The meeting's about t' start!"

Pulling the curtain across the closet, Bailey exited the room, wiping her eyes thoroughly before joining the others. Making her way out to the large room, she noted that John, Mike, and her uncle all sat in a ring of cushioned seats that appeared to have been carved out of the rock itself, smack in the middle of the enormous hall. Moving a chair from the closest dining table, she joined the others, who all sat in a larger circle around the smaller one, looking down upon their leaders.

"Ok," John's voice boomed, echoing off the walls. "Phase one is complete. We're settled in, an' everything looks good. However, it'd be perdy reckless o' us t' get too complacent. We gotta be on our toes, 'cause those bastards over in Pouty already attacked us once. We can damn well expect 'em t' do it again."

"Amen," one of the women in the outer ring concurred.

"That bein' said," the man continued, his eyes darting around at the members he could see, "we will get under way. Bailey!"

"Yes, sir!" the girl replied crisply, sitting up straighter in her seat.

"You're in charge o' the greenhouse! You need t' inventory our seed stock an' get that situated. See what pots are left an' if any o' them are usable. Within a week, we need the garden stock ready to sprout." He wafted a hand absently at the group. "You'll choose four o' the women to assist you."

"Yes, sir," she called again, already certain which four from the nice list she would be designating as her team.

"'Manda!" his voice continued to boom.

"Yes, sir!" the blonde replied from the far side of the room.

"Are you fit for duty?" his question blunt, he glared at the girl through narrowed slits.

"Uh," she faltered, shifting her gaze to Kathy for a moment. It had been only three weeks since the birth of her child, and although she wasn't a hundred percent, she damn sure had no intention of letting her community down. "Yes, sir," she replied as enthusiastically as she could muster. "I can lead the barn team."

"Good." He gave her a nod. "You get four o' the women as well. Alissa!"

"Yes, sir." Her hands twitched in her lap.

"You're in charge o' the kitchen an' household. You get everyone else o' the female persuasion." His mouth twisted into a crooked grin. "Caleb!"

"Yes, sir," he called with a snap in his voice.

"You got the stables, son, but you're on your own. We have t' keep the men rested for guard duty an' in case we're attacked. Can you handle it?"

"Yes, sir," the younger Cross responded confidently, unwilling to let his father down. "Could I recruit Carson at least?"

"That'd be fine," his father relented without argument. "You all set up your teams an' get th' details worked out. Dinner's in four hours, an' I wan' a report on where we stand from each o' you then! Meeting adjourned."

Exhaling a deep breath, Bailey stood, looking around for the girls she wanted to designate. Locating Amber, Judy, Lynette, and Rebecca, she gathered them around one of the large tables. "You guys are with me, right?" Flicking her gaze from face to face, she half expected them to say *no*.

When all of them had mumbled their agreement, the girl

smiled, ready to push on with greater confidence. "Great! I'm not even sure why he chose me! But thank you for your willingness to help."

"We don' really got a choice," Amber pointed out. "Everyone works in Lawson. If you don' work, you don' eat."

Bailey stared at her blankly for a moment, then grinned slightly. "Yes, well, I suppose you're right. Ok, let's get to the surface and see what's left up top."

With their new leader at the head of the pack, the group took the short stairs that led to the mid-level, which held all of the long term storage rooms Caleb had told her about. Having learned that the hallway ran east and west, with tunnels to the surface on both ends, she made a right. Arriving at the second set of stairs, they climbed and came out inside the safety of the tool shed that stood at one end of the greenhouse, closest to the ranch house.

Inside the long structure, the air would be warm enough for the group to work and move around without their jackets, provided everything was in order. Feeling that the air was cool but not frigid, Bailey grinned. "Well, that's a good sign."

Checking their drums of water, she began to give orders. "We'll need to get all of these filled. That will help with the temperature fluctuations."

"Yup," Rebecca agreed. "You want me t' take care of that now or when we finish?"

"When we finish." Bailey nodded at her friend. "Let's make a list for the moment." Looking around, she noticed that only a few of the tiles had been broken. "We need to find out if we have any replacement sections. Otherwise, we may need to cover them with plywood to keep out the excess wind. Where do you guys keep the pots when they're not in use?"

"I think they're in the end." Amber pointed at the storage on the opposite end from the entrance, closest to the Cross house.

Following her suggestion, Bailey opened the doors. "Well, thank God they didn't find these of any value." She smiled broadly at the shelves covered in various sized receptacles. "We need seeds, and we're all set."

"Those are gonna be under th' floor." Judy turned, kneeling down and wiping the dirt off of a small section. "If we had a broom, this part'd be easier."

Dropping to their knees beside her, the girls helped clear the area and rake the packed soil off of the wooden planks. They soon located the small holes that were used to grip the section and remove it. Once it had been pulled out of the way, Bailey gasped. "Oh my God. How long did it take you to collect these?"

The space was filled with small burlap bags, all stuffed with seeds for beans, tomatoes, okra, and the like. Lifting one, it measured about six inches square and weighed about a pound or two by her best estimate.

"We put back a bag every year." Rebecca wafted a hand over the collection. "An' there's two of each, the most recent years, stored below."

"Nice." Bailey nodded, flipping her long locks. "You guys are amazing! I love the way you always have a backup plan...for the backup plan," she praised her friends genuinely. Getting to her feet, she announced, "Ok, we need to clean up the mess that the Pouty people left. Then, Rebecca, you and Amber take care of restocking our water barrels. Judy, you and Lyn pull out the flats and start setting them up. I'm going to go find out about our compost."

Pulling on her jacket and taking a spade, Bailey hoped this would qualify as official business, as they would need to pull from the compost piles to make their soil mixture. Keeping the directive in mind, she kept to the edge of the field, where her footprints would be the most difficult to notice. Crunching through the snow, she grew sad for a moment, recalling how much Martha had shared with her and how much she had learned about the process over the last summer.

Arriving at the row of boxes that lay against the outer wall of the compound, Bailey used the hand tool to clear the snow out of the way and swung the door open, her heart beginning to beat faster with excitement. *Wow, we have plenty!*

Returning the cover to the tub, she cleared the rest of the row and called it good.

Making her way to rejoin her team, an odd sensation of peace came over her.

The simplicity of knowing her job—*my purpose*, she pondered as she picked her way through the drifts. *There's something to be said for the honesty and self-awareness of this place.*

Reaching the structure, an odd notion entered her thoughts. *I actually like being here!* There had been little in her life that brought her legitimate joy, and it was a real shame that the world had to face disaster in order for her to find it. *But if Jase and Jess were here to share in it, this would almost be like...heaven.*

Re-entering the greenhouse, she announced loudly, "We have plenty of compost, and the sand bucket is about three-quarters full. All we need is the seasoned soil, which is currently covered in a couple of feet of snow, and we're good to go."

"We'll have t' dig it out," Amber lamented.

"Right. I'm hoping one of the men will volunteer to help with that, but if not, we'll manage."

"How many o' these trays do we wanna lay out? We have more than enough." Lyn pointed at their selection.

Bailey recalled that the flats, as they were called, were the starter containers for the seeds. *After they have sprouted, we need to move them to pots.* "How many pots will we have? There's no sense starting too many of the seedlings if we won't have enough room to house them at the next stage."

Taking a quick count, they discovered that the pots were also in large supply. *Sweet.* "Ok, we can fill all these and get the seeds started. And actually, I would like to get them going as soon as possible so tomorrow morning, we start digging that soil out bright and early." She flitted her gaze around the faces of her crew. "But for now, I think we're set, so let's get downstairs and see what's for dinner."

The group, eager to get below and really settle in, chattered amicably in the passages.

Arriving at the great hall, they split to go their separate ways, and Bailey made her way to her new bedroom. *The one I will share with Caleb.*

The idea set loose a swarm of butterflies in her belly, and her feeling of happiness seemed to have her walking on air despite all the dark clouds around them.

SEVENTEEN

Practice Makes Perfect

BAILEY ARRIVED in her new quarters walking on sunshine despite the depth of the snow up top. Enjoying a quick shower, she removed the dirt and grime she had acquired cleaning out and setting up the greenhouse, and her mind continued to pour over her new assignment while she dressed. *I really wish the structure were twice the size.*

Having the large field had been useful when they had warm weather for a proper growing season, but the abrupt change in it could be more than a fluke. *If it continues, we may need more space for growing crops in a protected environment.*

Brushing out her long auburn tresses, she left her hair wet to dry naturally and made her way out into the great hall. Seeing that one of the tables already had the *menfolk*, along with Amanda and Caleb seated at it, deep in discussion, she felt a brief moment of panic. *I hope I'm not late!*

Pulling out a chair next to her blond-headed companion, she gave him a quick smile. "Sorry, guys. I didn't realize you were ready to begin."

"It's quite all right," Peter offered from the head of the table, taking charge of the evening's briefing. "We need to get our plates, and then we can really get down to business."

Making a quick trip through the serving line they had set up on one of the other three tables, the group took their seats for the second time, with Alissa taking the chair next to Bailey. Giving the older girl a grin, Bailey complimented, "Dinner looks fabulous!"

"It sure does." Her brown eyes shone with pride. "I wanted to make sure our first meal put everyone at ease. I'm sure this won' be an easy transition for us."

"That's good thinking," Bailey praised her friend, casting a quick glance around at the gathering. Deciding to dive in, she inquired, "So, did everyone have a good day all around?"

"Pretty much." Caleb pushed his leg over to brush against hers under the table. "I'm pretty set as far as th' horses go. We lost two in th' whole abduction thing, but the ones we got back are strong. An' the colt is doin' well, which is a relief."

"Star?" Her lip quivered slightly at the name her brothers had given the pony.

"Yup." He caressed the back of her right hand with an extended digit.

Seeing her discomfort, Peter took over. "How are the barn animals, Amanda?"

"Well, we don' have enough at the moment. We got the rabbits back, an' with some breeding, their population will return, so we'll have 'em as a meat source. But that's gonna get old," she summarized.

"Are they healthy?"

"Yeah, they seem to be doin' all right. We got all the other stalls cleaned out an' ready, so when we get some other livestock, they'll have a home. We'll need t' rebuild the chicken coop, since they totally destroyed the inside of ours for some reason. We're gonna have a few repairs t' make t' the barn, too, but other than that, we're good," she concluded.

"Good." Pete turned to Alissa. "I assume the meal is an indication that it's all going smoothly in housekeeping?"

"Yes." Alissa reached for a notepad she had placed on the table next to her in the empty spot to her left. Handing it to the man next to her, she indicated the list. "We only have two washing machines an' dryers down here, so we will need a schedule o' who will be laundered on which days."

Peter nodded, folding back the sheet. "Wow, you did all this... an' cooked!"

"Well, I do have help. An' it was easier for us, since this place didn't get trashed by those asshats while they were here." She grinned.

"Agreed." John held out his hand, accepting the tablet from his co-leader while smiling at the young woman across from him. "You did good, Alissa."

"Yes, you did, so finalize your rotation then so that everyone has their assignments," Peter finished off, ready to get to what his niece would contribute. "How's the greenhouse?"

"Fantastic, actually." Bailey swallowed her bite and washed it down with a swig of water. "We pulled out the trays, and I checked on the compost. We would love some help clearing a patch of ground for our seasoned soil if a few of the men wouldn't mind shoveling about a ten- or fifteen-foot section of snow, but other than that, we'll be good to go."

"And the structure?"

"A few minor repairs will be in order. And we might use a space heater to bring up the temperature, at least initially. Once we have everything sealed properly, with the water barrels we recharged today, it should be fairly easy to maintain." She cut her eyes over at the thus far silent man seated across from her tentatively.

Nodding at her, Michael grinned. "I guess you learned quite a bit from ol' Martha."

"Yes, sir." She swallowed visibly, nervous that they may have been testing her.

Picking up on her discomfort, Peter chuckled. "You did fine, little bit. Do you need anything else?"

"No, sir." She met his gaze. "I think we're as ready as we will be."

"All right. Be sure to inform us right away if anything changes." He pushed his empty plate back. "I guess we are adjourned. You guys can go as soon as you're finished eating."

Polishing off their meal eagerly, Caleb rose and offered her his hand, smiling brightly when she took it and accompanied him to their chamber. Closing the door behind them, he spun her around in a twirl and planted her against the wall. His arms locked, palms flat against the smooth surface on either side of her head, his smile morphed into something more like a sneer. "Did you miss me?"

"Of course." Her hand moved to his chest, fingers sliding lightly over his ribs. "I was worried you would overdo it today. How do you feel?"

"Like I could walk on water." His body dropped, his arms folding enough to bring them face to face. "I couldn' get you outta my head."

Raising her face to touch her lips to his, she exhaled a long, slow breath through her nose. Pushing lightly against him, she whispered, "I have something I need to tell you."

Picking up on the tension in her body, he relaxed, allowing about six inches of air between them. "Ok. I'm listenin'." He felt a stab of fear at what she might divulge.

Her green eyes wide, she stared at him, her pulse loud in her ears. "I think I love you," she managed in the strongest voice she could muster, which turned out hardly audible.

"Wow, don't sound so excited." He pushed further away from her, slightly disappointed in her weak admission.

"I'm sorry," she stammered. "I told you. My family was never big on this sort of thing!"

"Oh." He recalled their previous conversations. "So I guess that's the best you can do?"

"Well, yes! And it's not like you've been over the top professing your devotion!" She heard the twinge of anger in her voice and immediately back pedaled. "I'm sorry. It's not right for me to shout at you."

He showed her his full set of perfect white teeth. "You mean you don' know?"

"No, I don't," she clipped, laying her head against the wall behind her.

"I'm crazy about you, Bailey." He leaned in to nuzzle her face, his lips finding her ear. "I love you more than I can say. I need you more than anything else I can think of. More than food…more than water…maybe even more than th' air that I breathe."

She giggled, her hands pushing lightly on his chest.

"What?" He allowed her a bit of room. "Is that not what you wanted t' hear?"

"I don't know." Her hand found his chin. "I've never been like this with anyone, so this is all new to me. I'm not sure what I want, except to make you happy."

"Me too." His grin twisted. "But I like it!" Dropping his hands, he fumbled for her clothing, ready to strip her down and have his way with her. Eager to please him, she gave no argument, helping to remove them so they could get down to business.

Lying in the darkness with him after his hunger had been satisfied, Bailey sighed loudly.

Petting her bare skin with his large hands, Caleb picked up on her distant mood. "Wha's the matter, baby?" his words cut through her scattered thoughts.

"Nothing," she replied listlessly. "You obviously enjoy it, and I guess that's what matters."

Pushing himself up onto an elbow, he stared down at her in the dim light that filtered under their door. "Whadda you mean? You don' like it?" he demanded incredulously.

"I didn't say that," she lied flatly. Inhaling deeply, she didn't want to hurt his feelings and exhaled through tight lips. "It's just not like what I thought it would be."

"Yeah, me either," he confessed.

"That's nice to know," she bit with a stab of displeasure, afraid she had let him down somehow. "I guess Amanda was a better lover."

He blinked at her, his jaw hanging open before he clamped it shut. "I wouldn't know. I've never been with her. Or anyone else, for that matter." He sounded hurt.

Bolting straight up, as if he had punched her, Bailey snapped on the light mounted to the wall. "What do you mean you've never been with anyone else?"

Running his hand through his blond spikes, he sat up next to her. "Exactly that. You weren' the only one waitin' for th' right person," he admitted. "So if I'm not doin' a good job, I need t' find out how t' do it better. I mean"—he grinned—"I think it's great, an' I love it. But you gotta think so too, or tha's no good."

Bailey stared at him, her mind racing. *Holy shit! He's never slept with anyone but me?* The depth of that concept almost more than she could fathom, she quipped accusingly, "Why would you do that? Not ever…before? I thought guys were always ready and willing…" Her voice faded.

He shrugged, her tone making him uncomfortable. "What, like cheerleaders?" he huffed, not meeting her glare. Shifting to ensure he was covered by adjusting the sheet, he stated firmly, "No, baby, you're not the only one with ideals or beliefs. I wanted it t' be special, same as you. One girl that'd be mine for all my life. An' Amanda…wadn' it."

He shook his head when he spoke of the other woman, pulling his knees to his chest and wrapping his arms around them. Turning his face to meet her silent green-eyed stare, his voice became a loud whisper. "I was waiting for you, Bailey. You're my one an' only."

Rolling her tongue around for a moment, she considered his words before she said anything else that might make things worse. "I'm sorry. That was insensitive of me."

"It's ok." He shrugged, fingering a long section of auburn locks that dangled across her chest. "I didn't tell you. Maybe I should have."

"Well, we did kind of get pushed into this." She leaned forward, kissing him lightly. "So we'll get better at it together."

"Oh, you know"—he chuckled, tucking her beneath him —"practice makes perfect." His body sliding roughly across hers, he began to pant. "I really do love you, Bailey. From the depths o' my soul."

"I love you, too," she breathed against the hollow of his neck. Moving to make it easier for him, she wanted him to be happy; the realization he wanted the same for her made it all the more incredible.

EIGHTEEN

A New World Order

"NICE," Bailey commented aloud to Lyn, who had been helping her replant their first crop of seedlings. "I can't believe how many of these sprouted!"

"I know," the girl agreed. "This could be the healthiest start I've ever seen. You definitely got a green thumb."

"I had help." The taller girl grinned with pride. "But I can't say I'm not pleased with the result."

Cutting her blue eyes over at her boss, she flicked her soft brown waves. "Someday we're gonna get that uptight way you talk worked out!" Her words holding a small sting, her laughter lessened the blow.

"Sorry." Bailey flushed slightly. "I know I don't really fit in here all that well."

"Bullshit," Amber joined the conversation. "You fit in enough. So when are you an' Caleb gonna have a real weddin'?"

"I don't really know." The girl dropped the conversation to retrieve more pots. When she returned, she pointed out bluntly, "Caleb hasn't actually asked me to marry him. And I have to admit, with the way the world is changing, I don't know that he will."

"Sure he will," Lyn scoffed. "He's an ol' fashioned kinda guy, after all. I'm surprised he didn't insist on it before you guys moved in together."

"Well, we didn't really have a choice, since we made the move into Lawson." She glanced out the open window at the melting snow. "But I'm sure it will remain so even after we move back to the houses."

"You think we will?" Judy called from across the building, having been listening quietly while she worked. "Livin' in the ground ain't any fun at all."

"I know," Bailey agreed, "but the melt scares me a little. Luis and Connie have not returned, and I'm afraid Pouty may be waiting for the right time to attack us. If the *menfolk* feel the same way, we won't make the move anytime soon."

"They wouldn't attack us," Amber speculated. "They would get their asses kicked, an' they know it."

"I don't know about that," Bailey persisted, wiping the sweat from her brow. "We have a new world order, and survival of the fittest is definitely in play." Wafting her hand over their completed work, she smiled. "At least we have the skills and means to get by even if the rest of humanity falls away."

"We're not the only ones," Amber insisted. "There's gotta be other people."

"Oh, I'm sure there are." Bailey grimaced, leading the way to the passage below. "The problem is, will they be our friends or foes when we meet. I, for one, wish that Pouty could have been our allies instead of our enemies. But when resources are scarce, that's what you get."

Reaching the main hall, the young women headed for the serving line and made their plates, choosing to sit together and continue their conversation. A few of the other girls joined them, including Amanda. Seeing how tired the girl appeared, Bailey felt her heart go out to her.

"How're you doing? You look beat." She hoped she wasn't being too forward.

"I am," the taller girl admitted. "Hope still ain't sleepin' through the night, an' that's wearin' on me. I can only imagine what that's gonna be like when we get th' barn restocked an' we're runnin' at full capacity."

"Any idea when that's going to happen?" Bailey glanced around, noticing that none of the men had come down yet. "Where is everyone?" she changed the subject abruptly.

"I think they're plannin' sumthin'," Amber pointed out. "Mom's pretty upset Dad never came home, an' she's been buggin' them t' do sumthin' about it."

"You mean we're going to attack Pouty?" Bailey's mouth hung open. "When?"

"I dunno." She shook her ebony locks, lowering her voice. "But I can try t' find out."

"Yeah," Rebecca agreed, spearing green beans with her fork. "She's good at that sorta thing."

Noticing Amanda's expression, Bailey suspected some of them already knew. When their eyes met, all doubt was removed. "What do you know?"

"I don' really know anything." The lanky blonde licked her lips nervously, again scanning the chamber. "Not fur sure, anyhow. But night before last, Don an' Dev went on a little recon. Took one o' the Jeeps fur a little ride. The main road's completely thawed, an' that's got 'em all in an uproar. They say we need t' strike first before Pouty gets the chance."

"Wow." Kristen's eyes grew wide. "I don't see how takin' that risk's gonna help us!"

"It's not fur us t' decide," Amanda corrected. "It's always been up t' th' *menfolk* to run things."

"But the *menfolk* has changed," Judy spoke up. "There's only three o' them now, an' no offense, but I ain't sure they know as much t' do as when Jim was here. He was a smart ol' man, an' he took good care o' us."

"My uncle will, too," Bailey defended her relation. "Besides, it's a community say, and none of them are really in charge."

"That's the point," the other girl countered. "Used to be we had seven heads t' do th' thinkin'. Now we only got three. Not so much smarts."

"So maybe it's time some of the younger men joined the *menfolk*." The rest of the girls stared at her as if she had sprouted horns on the top of her head. "What? It could be done. In fact, it should be done! They are a part of this too, and we need wise counsel!" Giving the rest an angry glare, the outburst brought the conversation to an abrupt halt, leaving a bad taste in the girl's mouth.

Finishing their meal, the group disbanded and returned to their chores for a few more hours. Back up top, Bailey had an uneasy feeling in the pit of her stomach. Standing in the wide doorway as the sun moved to set, she watched the ice melting from the bare tree limbs in the orchard. Listening to the water drip, almost enough to sound like rain, her mind drifted back to the week of her parents' funeral.

We're in trouble, she admitted to herself internally. *If the roads are clearing, it won't be long and Pouty will come for us.* The fact that the others had not joined them, and further that Luis and Connie had not returned, appeared to be a bad omen. *Jess and Jase are lost, maybe forever.*

Wiping at her tears, she hoped no one had noticed her sorrow. No one had spoken to her since her tantrum during lunch, and she could hardly blame them. *I'm still new to all this survivalist crap… but I guess in a way we all are.*

Trudging down the steps alone, it pleased her to see that the men were all downstairs for the evening, save Don, who was probably on guard duty at the gate. *Of course, that's part of my point.* They had been standing guard for the entire month that they had been living underground, and no one had seen anything moving beyond their walls.

Bailey had also snuck over to the Cross house a few times during that time to check the internet, but the signal had not returned, nor did any of their phones have service. *We're cut off from the rest of the world, and the only thing worse than knowing about what is going on...is not knowing.*

Locating Caleb, she plunked down into the seat next to him, placing her plate on the table loudly. Giving her a sideways glance, he grinned. "What's up, baby? You seem like somethin's wrong."

"No." She frowned at her food, her appetite somewhat diminished. "Not really, I guess. I have this feeling something isn't right. That's all."

"Of course it's not right." He brushed the auburn curtain out of the way so he could see her profile. "We're livin' in a hole in the ground. But the weather appears t' be breakin', an' that's a good sign."

Lifting her eyes, she stared at him. "Tell me the truth, Caleb. You said you would never lie to me, so please don't start now."

"Aww, baby." He half-smiled. "You remember that I'm always lookin' out for you, right?"

"Yes, I know. And you will tell me when I'm ready to hear," she finished for him.

"Right." He slid his arm around her, pulling her against his chest. "So let me do the worryin', an' you take care o' growin' food an' takin' care o' things like that."

Lifting her gaze, she stared at him. "Make sure you tell me before you do anything dangerous...or stupid. I'd like to have some warning before I lose anyone else that I care about..." Her voice squeaked by the time she finished speaking, her chin quivering.

His fingers grazed her cheek lightly. "You're not gonna lose me, baby. I promise."

"You can't promise me that," she countered swiftly. "No one can. And I've lost too many people to pretend that you could." Standing, she left her plate where it sat, walking away from him and taking the short flight of stairs to the mid-level and on to the barn.

As soon as she was out in the cool evening air, she felt better. Patches came bounding over to see her, and she greeted the momma dog cheerfully with a firm scratch behind the ears. "How's my girl tonight?"

The three pups bounced around her as she knelt to stroke their mother. "Hey, fellas," she greeted Brownie, Blackie, and Spot with a bit of rough play. Giggling at the trio, she jumped slightly when Caleb appeared out of nowhere. "Holy shit! Make some noise next time!"

Laughing, he quibbled, "An' where's the fun in that?" accepting her playful punch to the arm. "I'm glad these guys survived." He lifted Brownie to toy with. "Although Carson's choice in names coulda been better."

"Their names are fine." She actually sat on the ground, allowing them to climb into her lap. "I think they suit them, and that's what you said. You know, you never did tell me about your other dogs. The ones you had before."

"Nope." He held the pup above him towards the light, grinning at the way it squirmed before he too sat and placed it in his lap. "It's a sad story, little bit. Don' really think you wanna hear it, especially tonight."

"No, I do!" she demanded with wide eyes. "Really. Please share!"

Giving her a doubtful glare, he kept his focus on the tiny animals, giving Patches a stroke as well when she curled up in front of them and flicked her tail. "Ok." He sighed. "But jus' remember, I warned you."

"Yes." She grinned. "I've been warned."

Playing with the young animal in his folded legs, he began, "When I was about eight, your uncle an' aunt had finished th' ranch house an' were movin' into it. On one o' their trips t' buy furniture, he brought back two pups an' gave them t' me."

Bailey smiled. "Awww. This was before Carson was born?"

"Yeah." He nodded. "The year before. Anyways, I named them Dan an' Anne—"

"Where the Red Fern Grows!" she interrupted him, and he grinned broadly.

"Yeah. I loved the book an' thought it was a great idea." His features shifted at the memory. "In hindsight, it was a bad move," he admitted, watching her brow furrow. "By the time I was twelve, I had figured out my ol' man was a mean son of a bitch. Thought I was gonna stand up t' him an' change all our lives for the better. He didn' like my attitude…" His voice trailed away.

"So"—he drew a deep breath—"he an' I get int' a shoutin' match one night, an' I really tell him off. Then he gets this wicked grin on his face an' tells me I need a lesson I won' never forget. He grabs my dogs an' hauls them out in front o' the house"—his eyes bore into hers—"one by one…an' he shoots them both in the back o' th' head." He used his fingers to illustrate on the small bundle of fur in his lap.

"Holy shit!" Bailey breathed, the air caught in her lungs as if she had been kicked. "What happened?"

"He made me bury 'em." Caleb shrugged, his eyes misty. "An' here I am twenty-two years ol' an' I still wanna cry when I think about 'em!" He looked over at her, blinking rapidly, the red ring around his lids a neon sign of his emotional state.

"Aww, honey." She flung her arms around him. "I'm so sorry! I shouldn't have asked!" Caressing the nape of his neck, she sniffled, battling with her own tears.

"No." He pulled her closer, hugging her tightly. "It's ok. It feels good t' share my stories with you…even the sad ones." After a long moment, she sank back into her spot, and he continued, "Anyways, I never challenged him again. Not once, until that night he slapped you upside the head. He's sure as fuck lucky I had wrapped an' cracked ribs or I woulda dragged his ass outside for damn sure."

"No you wouldn't have!"

"I sure as hell would have." He grimaced. "I was livid an' tol' him he won' ever lay a hand on you again, an' I damn sure meant it."

"Like Ked," she panted. "That night he jumped me."

"Yeah, like him." He wiped his nose on his sleeve. "I can't let anything happen to you, little bit. You're my whole world an' have been for a long time now."

"It won't." She grinned.

"You can't promise me that," he mocked her, then raised a hand to trace her jaw. "I'm just as scared o' losin' you as you are o' losin' me. But we have t' do somethin' or we won' ever be safe. Pouty has t' be dealt with, an' we need t' get our people back if we can."

"Agreed." She nodded, ready to call it a night. Standing, she waited for him to join her at the door. Cutting off the light, he flipped on his hand held, and the couple made their way below.

NINETEEN

Comforts of Home

CALEB LAY IN THE DARKNESS, listening to the silence of the cave. His arm draped over Bailey's chest, the sound of her soft breath was the only thing he could hear. *I never realized how much noise the world makes...even out away from other people.* They had made love again that night, and true to his word, he had been getting better at pleasuring her. Hugging her a little tighter, he sighed. "I love you so much, little bit."

Stirring slightly at his voice, he grinned into the back of her head, then froze. Outside their door, he could hear shouts echoing through the rock caverns. Leaping out from the covers, he grabbed his jeans and yanked them on.

"What's going on?" her tone sounded groggy.

"Nothin'," he soothed. "Get some rest. I'll be back in a minute," grabbing his shirt and boots. Then he left her there, closing the door quietly behind him.

Lying alone for a long moment, the fact that he had departed unexpectedly put her mind to work, and sleep soon became a moot point. When he hadn't returned in what seemed an eternity, she climbed out of the bed and donned her own clothing, muttering, "What the hell, what the hell, what the hell," to herself.

Out in the main hall, things were quiet, but there were several other women gathered in the kitchen. Entering the room, Bailey noted they were making coffee. "What's going on?"

"You should go back to bed," Paula informed her crisply. "Leave this to the adults."

"Uh, I am one of the adults, thank you very much," Bailey shot back. "I'm in charge of the greenhouse. So what's going on?"

The other woman glared at her, while Deanna frowned. "You know, we like you well enough. An' we've come to accept that you're not leavin'. But you're still one o' the kids."

"So what?" Amanda stepped into the room. "Kids grow up. What's goin' on, Mom?" She cut her mother a spiteful glare.

Drawing a deep breath, the woman glanced at the other, then sighed. "The guys are up top. Someone showed up at the gate in a Jeep."

"Oh my God!" Bailey gasped. "From Pouty?" Her pulse hammered in her ears, a mixture of excitement and fear.

"We don' know anything yet. The *menfolk* will decide what t' do, and then we will be told," she reluctantly supplied. "Go take care o' Hope, baby. We'll let you know when we get word."

Amanda frowned. "She's asleep, Mom, an' I got th' door open, so I can hear if she cries." Turning to Bailey, she grinned faintly. "Wanna grab some cups an' go sit in th' pit?"

"Sure." The slender young woman nodded. "I'd like that." She and the other girl had slowly been learning about one another and had reached the point of almost being friends. "You can bring Hope out with us if you like."

"After she wakes up." Amanda gathered their mugs. "She's got another hour or so before that happens."

Accepting the warm liquid, the pair made their way out to the circle in the center of the great hall. Climbing down onto the cushioned seat, Bailey tucked her feet beneath her, yawning in an exaggerated manner. To her surprise, Jennifer joined them, and she noted the bump in her midsection had grown large enough to be obvious.

Amanda grinned. "How long before yur baby comes?"

Jennifer rubbed her belly. "Guess it's startin' t' show, huh? Still a long time." She grinned. Her eyes darting over at Bailey, she giggled. "You're next, ya know?"

Shaking her auburn waves, Bailey snapped, "No way! Not me!" Her mind instantly darted to the box of condoms Caleb had left sitting on the table in the med center. "Oh God, you think so?"

"Sure do." Amanda grinned as well, taking a noisy sip from her mug. Noticing her husband come in from the armory stairs, she sat up straight. "Oh, shit!" Getting to her feet, she called to him as he crossed in front of the kitchen, headed to their quarters. "DEV!"

Pivoting, he grinned, adjusting his course. Turning to the two men who followed behind, he wafted, "Dey already awake."

"O' course they are." Caleb climbed down into the pit and flopped onto the cushion next to Bailey's stiff frame. "Fancy seeing the three o' you together, chattin' like ol' friends."

The girls exchanged a glance before Amanda took charge. "So wha's goin' on?"

Don took the seat next to Jennifer, informing them, "That girl showed up at the gate last night."

"What girl?" Bailey demanded loudly.

"Dat girl, da one Luis brought over here." Devon dropped his arm around his bride. "An' da *menfolk's* gonna give us a vote what t' do wit 'er. Us an' Nung."

"Oh my God." Her green eyes shone as she cut them over at the man next to her. "They're making you part of the leadership?"

"I guess so." Caleb shrugged. "About time, if you ask me. Th' problem is, they want us t' help decide what t' do about the girl."

"Well, why's she here?" Jen queried, her tone almost angry. "She came alone? Didn' even bring none o' our people with her?"

"No." He massaged his stubble-covered chin. "An' she's not sayin' anything until we decide what we're gonna do with her. Except that we're in danger an' Pouty's comin' t' get us."

"Well, that was a given." Bailey's brow furrowed above her green orbs. "What about our people?"

"Nope, not givin' up a thang," Devon stated emphatically. "But we need to decide how we're gonna vote."

"Vote for what?" she snapped, irritated at the lack of real information.

"Baby, you know my dad ain't got a problem knockin' a woman around. He wants t' torture her an' find out what she knows." His face appeared grave.

"No way." Bailey leapt to her feet. "I can't believe you even had to ask my opinion on this!"

Amanda gaped at her. "You hol' on a second. That girl cain't stay here! What if she's a spy? What if they sent her over here on purpose?"

"Then we take that chance! Don't you see? She came here. Luis brought her. Why isn't he with her?" She cut her eyes over at Caleb.

"She won' tell us anything." He sighed, running his fingers through his hair. He had already known what the girl would think, and having it confirmed in front of the others didn't make him feel any better about their choice. "You know how th' vote works."

"My uncle won't go for that. You think Mike would?" She glared at Don squarely. "You know this is where you show what kind of man you really are. If you hurt that girl, then you don't deserve to survive. Karma's a real bitch, and we will get what's coming to us, either way!"

Spinning around, she hoisted herself up and over the cushioned seat. Grasping her empty cup firmly, she slammed the door to her bedroom loudly. *I can't believe he is even considering hurting her!* Flopping across the bed, she bawled uncontrollably. *Please God. I don't ask for much. Please don't let them make the wrong choice.*

Staring after her while she made her retreat, Caleb emitted a loud sigh. "Damn, she's emotional! O' course, she grew up in a different place, so she don't see things the same way." Returning his attention to those remaining in the circle, he saw Jen and Amanda share a look. Pursing his lips, he coughed. "What?"

"Nothin'." The blonde shook her long, golden locks. "But ya

know you can't let anything happen t' Bonny. Your girlfriend may be overly emotional, but she's right."

"Agreed," Devon spoke up. "My vote." Glaring at Don, he waited to hear what he had to say.

Rubbing his palms on his jeans, the smaller man cast a glance at the girl seated next to him. "I knew comin' down here was a bad idea."

"What? You don' value our opinions? Ya know, that could be how half the *menfolk* ended up dead, not listenin' t' th' women," Jen quipped.

"Yeah, I doubt that." His eyes darted from face to face. Still, he knew she wouldn't be happy if he sentenced the girl to suffering… or worse. "But we're only three votes. One of them has to side with us or it don't matter what we think."

"Then we go do our best." Caleb got to his feet, shoving his hands in his pockets. "If Pete sides with us, it'll be enough. Either way, I'll be back in a bit. I'm not gonna hang around an' watch if they lay int' her." Climbing out, he headed for the stairs, ready to render his verdict, along with his counterparts.

Hearing the soft cry of her infant, Amanda curled a few fingers at her sister. "Time to feed. I swear I feel like a milk cow right now!"

The other girl giggled, following her into her quarters so she could care for her daughter. The feeding had just ended when the group of men came noisily through the entrance. Placing her babe against her shoulder and covering her with a light blanket, Amanda followed the shorter girl out into the great hall, grinning to herself when she noticed the young, ebony-haired woman in the midst of the men.

Hearing the ruckus, Bailey wiped at her eyes, her fear getting the better of her for a brief moment. Quickly deciding she had to know what had taken place either way, she climbed off the bed and stopped in the bathroom to wash her face before making her way outside.

The group had settled into the pit. All of the *menfolk*, seven strong once again, sat on the cushioned seats, while the rest had gathered chairs around the outer ring. With the men below sat a single female, her hands wrapped around a warm mug of coffee.

"Oh my God!" Bailey shrieked, dashing across the space and reaching her by bouncing down into the sunken area. "You're ok." She stroked the other girl's hair. "They didn't hurt you!"

Staring up at her with a stunned expression, Bonny swallowed noticeably. "Well, I guess that means they weren't bluffin', huh?"

"No, they weren't." Bailey knelt in front of her. "I'm so glad you're ok. Please, tell me about my brothers. About everyone! How are they?"

Licking her lips, the girl considered her options, still in awe of the massive underground cavern. "A lot of them are dead," she confessed, a few tears spilling over to drip from her jaw before she could wipe them away. "They killed Luis an' Connie as soon as we got there. One of them tried to kill me, too. Choked me unconscious, but someone stopped him before it was too late. I think it was Phil. He's the ringleader, but I guess you know that.

"I'm real sorry about your people." She stared at the floor. "A woman, Martha I think her name was, and the other guy, Chris... they caught them the night of the fire, and they beat them to death as well."

"Oh dear Lord." One of the older women began to sob. "My husband ain't comin' home!"

Bailey noticed the younger girls were not present, and she was glad of that. They had bad tidings coming, and she knew it would be hard on them. "What about the rest? My brothers and the girls?"

"I never laid eyes on them," she confessed. "But I think they're alive. They are at the commune, on the edge of town, where the fields start."

"You mean on that farm you guys were tryin' t' build?" John cut in, aware of only a few particulars of the town.

"Yeah, on the farm. They were sent there to help. I didn't know where they were before, an' I couldn't get to them now, to bring them with me"—she shuddered—"but I had to get over here before

148

it was too late. You guys are gonna get hit—tomorrow in fact. They're bringing everything they got to attack you!"

"Wow, all that over a few horses an' rabbits?" Peter muttered.

Staring at him with her mouth hanging open, Bonny stammered, "No, they were more pissed about the people you killed an' the buildings you destroyed!"

"Buildings?" His eyes darted over at Bailey. "We burned the police station. It was part of our escape, to keep them occupied while we got away," he stated matter-of-factly.

"Yeah, good plan," she bit angrily. "They couldn't put out the fire, and all of downtown burned to the ground! Dozens of people died, an' they ain't gonna let that lay." She glanced around the group. "And part of your food was bad. They think you poisoned them. Either way you slice it, they have an axe to grind against the whole mess of you."

"Oh my God," Bailey gasped. "Are you sure they didn't hurt my brothers? In retaliation?"

"I ain't sure of anything," the girl countered. "All I know is you better be ready 'cause they have every intention of putting every last man, woman, and child here in the ground an' takin' this place for themselves."

"They know about Lawson?" Mike demanded in surprise.

"What's Lawson?" she asked quietly, eyes full of fear.

"This," he bellowed, opening his right palm to indicate the space around them. "All o' this! Do they know?"

"No way." Her ebony locks shimmered when she shook them. "I didn't even know, an' I didn't tell them shit about this place on top of that! Trust me. They killed Luis." Her tears trickled unchecked. "The last thing I would do is help *them*."

"All right," John took charge. "Then we need t' get ready. Get us some grub, ladies, so we can eat while we formulate our plan."

TWENTY

Who's the Man

GETTING TO HIS FEET, the senior Cross glared around at the group. "Gentlemen, let's move to a table, an' we're gonna need some paper t' make some sketches."

"I guess you think you're in charge," Pete challenged. "Or do we all get a say?"

"I figure we'll all contribute our ideas an' pick the best one." John stood up straighter. "However, I do have actual combat experience, same as you. So don't go thinkin' you know more 'an I do."

"Look, we ain't got time to argue about who's in charge around here," Caleb interceded. "They'll be here in a few hours, worst case scenario." He glanced over at the girl. "Any idea when?"

"No." She shook her head. "I only know they were making the preparations yesterday."

"Then like I said, we don' got time t' fight amongst ourselves. We're outnumbered an' maybe even outgunned, so we need a good plan that we can all get behind." He put his hands on his hips as he rebuked them.

Standing next to him, Bailey ran her hand up and down his arm. "Is it going to be like before?" her voice trembled slightly.

"Yeah." He nodded, placing his hand in hers. "You girls all

learned t' shoot for a reason, an' we're gonna need us all if we're gonna survive."

Bailey stared at the floor in front of her, giving his hand a squeeze. "Ok." Dropping the appendage, she climbed out of the pit and strolled over to the bookcase outside her quarters, where a stack of legal-sized notepads had been stored, presumably for the younger members to use while they were homeschooled. Turning to the closest table, she set out ten spots, including pens, and stared at the group of men.

"When did you earn the right t' sit with the *menfolk?*" John demanded, stepping up to the top level. "This ain't runnin' the garden! Or any other silly ass girlie shit!"

Bailey clenched her jaw. "I guess the day I shot a man in the head. Or the day they stole my brothers. You take your pick." Pulling out a chair, she took a seat, crossing her hands over the bright yellow page.

Skirting the flat surface and taking the chair next to her, Caleb also sat down. "I didn't actually tell them about that," he stated in a low tone.

"Didn't tell us about what?" Peter shuffled forward, resting his arms on the back of a chair opposite the couple. "Come on. What the hell's she talking about?"

"On our way out here, during the first blizzard"—Caleb shifted uncomfortably—"some guys from the gas station followed us. Seven o' them, anyways. I took out six o' them, an' Bailey got the other one."

"You shot a man?" Her uncle glared at her.

"He cornered me." She raised her chin defiantly. "I tried to hide, and he found me. He didn't leave me any choice."

John laughed loudly. "Take a seat, fellas. 'Manda, you sit, too. We need t' decide exactly how we're gonna go about this, an' we're gonna need all o' us t' execute the plan."

Once everyone was seated, the group began to hash out scenarios. Mike suggested they hide and attack the group when they came into the compound. "Like a reverse Trojan Horse."

Although he seemed excited, the option received all negative commentary.

Devon wanted to use the helicopter to mount a counter offensive, thinking they could fashion some type of sticky bombs to drop on what was left of their buildings. This also was not a well thought of plan. Eating their early breakfast, the group continued, not able to come to anything conclusive.

Listening to them talk, Bonny inched her way closer, little by little. Eventually, she spoke up. "You know, you guys only have that one road to get here."

"Yup," Don agreed. "That's why I think we should line up along the wall an' just shoot their asses when they come up. We have not one but *two* RPGs in the storage for such an occasion." He held up two fingers in a V to emphasize the point.

"We don't want to damage the road. Like you said, it's the only one we got, an' if we tear it up, we're screwed. We already lost our gate," Mike countered.

Peter dug his fingers into his sandy salt and pepper curls, his frustration punctuated by a loud groan. "We need something simple. RPGs are not gonna cut it. An' if we line up on the wall, we could become the targets. An' they can't come in the front gate because we sealed it."

"So what *can* they do?" Bailey asked, sounding distant. "I mean, how are they going to get here?"

Subconsciously, everyone in the group shifted their gaze to the new girl. Nodding, she sighed. "They have several SUVs they were loading down with everything that they could round up from the houses. But I can't help thinking if they're comin' over here, that would be the perfect time to attack them. Or at least get those kids back."

John stared at her, breathing loudly through his mouth. "You're sure all they got's some SUVs? No other aircraft or a tank or anything?"

"Maybe some pickup trucks." The girl grinned at him. "But nothin' that would be much else. They used your CAT to tear down

153

your fence when they were here before, but they only did that 'cause no one would give them the code to open it."

"How do you know that?" Caleb eyed her warily.

"They talked about it at th' diner." She shrugged. "That's one o' the first things Phil wanted to take when they were able to get back over here after the snow ended."

Staring at her, Bailey's green eyes lit up. "I think you're right. We should go get our people back while they're over here."

"An' how do we do that? There aren't enough o' us to split our forces." John slapped the table.

"Sure there are." The girl grinned deviously. "You said you didn't want to tear up the road. So make them get off of it, and then blow them up."

"An' how do we do that?" Caleb leaned back in his chair, his hand absently reaching for a few strands of auburn hair to play with.

"We block the road. Use the Jeep those assholes from the gas station drove over here. It's still parked in the pasture. If you can't drive it, use the CAT to drag it around there, and if anything happens to it we haven't lost anything. Put it far enough out, they will pull off the road to go around...and blow them up." She shrugged at the simplicity of her plan.

"How does that get our people back?" Pete leaned forward, intrigued by her train of thought. "We have a helicopter and an airplane. Between the two of them, I bet we could get over there and back in no time. You know where they are, right?"

"Yeah." Bonny reached for one of the notepads, moving between Don and Peter as she did so. "This is the town." She began to sketch. "Over here, we have three farms set up, one that's got all your animals on it. The boys are there. These other two are for crops, and the girls are there, at this one." She circled the last box on her sketch.

"Man, dat plan's anythin' but simple," Devon spoke for the first time in a while.

"Yeah, but I like it." John's smile went from ear to ear. "Are we takin' only the people, or do we try t' get more o' our animals back?"

"We could haul them in the horse trailer if we had to, but we would need t' get it outta here an' stash it some place until we were ready for it." Caleb tapped Bonny's map. "I'd love to get a load o' the hogs an' chickens back."

"Wouldn't we all." Peter nodded. "But we have no way o' communicating, since they snatched all the radio equipment. Too bad we didn't have any back-ups o' those hidden in Lawson. An' we don't really have a hiding place for a truck an' trailer, as it is."

"Wouldn't o' mattered," John announced. "The handhelds had a limited range, so they only worked house t' house anyways. If they're gonna hide, it's gotta be further away than that."

"What about the gas station?" Bailey suggested quietly. When everyone only stared at her she continued. "There was only one other guy there that we saw that didn't come here. Even if there's more, there can't be that many. Besides, we could take Caleb's bike back if it's still there."

The blond-headed man began to laugh. "Son of a bitch. Wouldn't that be funny? I'm down for that! I'll go hook up the horse trailer, an' Bailey can go with me, along with Don or Nung. You pick."

"I'm goin', too." Amanda stood. "I can help with the animals, an' we'll take a few cages with us jus' in case."

"So John an' I set up the roadblock an' take out their vehicles," Mike suggested, "while Devon an' Pete take the helicopter an' plane over to Pouty."

"Yeah, but they shouldn't take off until the vehicles are wiped out. That way, if somethin' goes wrong, you guys can adjust the plan," Caleb stipulated. "But I still don' see how we're gonna know when t' go."

"I guess we could keep an eye out," Bailey suggested. "When we see them take off or fly over, we can join them. It'll take us a bit longer to get there, but not too much longer. But where are you going to land the plane? Do they have an air strip?"

"No." Bonny shook her head. "No strip. Just a pad for the helicopter outside of town."

"Oh, that's perfect! We go land on their pad an' show up in their truck, they'll think the fights over an' their guys are bringing their stuff back!" Pete beamed. "An' don't worry about the airplane. I'm sure I can land on the road there somewhere. It's a smaller model an' don't need much of a runway, but I bet I can still get all four of the kids in with me as well."

Slapping the table, John got to his feet. "Hot damn, guys an' dolls, we need t' get movin' so we can be ready when they get here. Nung, you go with the kids an' set up over at the garage. We'll get some o' these girls on the wall with rifles, too. They're all good shots, an' when push comes to shove, we may need the extra fire power. Oh, an' in case anyone has any doubts, any an' all that get in our way, will be KOS."

"Kill on sight," Caleb echoed grimly. "Sounds fair. I'm sure they aren't on their way over to take everyone prisoner again."

"Uh, no." Bonny shook her ebony curls. "They intend to kill everyone here."

"Then we got no problem returning the favor," Peter agreed as he stood. "I'll go see about gettin' that Jeep taken care of. You all have your jobs. Let's move!"

Turning to Bailey, Caleb gave her a wry grin. "Sorry, little bit. I think I volunteered you for the most dangerous part."

"You're going to help get my brothers back. There's no other job I would rather have." She giggled, leaning forward to give him a peck on the lips. "I really don't think you could have kept me away."

TWENTY-ONE

Broken

BAILEY CLIMBED into the back seat of the truck, closing the half-door behind her. "How long before sunrise?"

"At least an hour," Nung supplied, taking the passenger seat in front of her. Glancing over at the tall blonde who sat behind Caleb, he scowled. "You sure leaving your child alone is a good idea?"

"Momma's watchin' her. Hell, she's mosta the reason I'm goin'. It's her future we're fightin' for, as well as our own."

"Amen," Caleb agreed, starting the truck and pulling out of the gate. As soon as they passed through it, Mike rolled it shut behind them, and they followed the outer wall to the front of the compound. On the paved road, they would be able to increase their speed, as the snow and ice were completely gone.

"When we get to the station, we may get problems," he cautioned. "We killed their friends, an' I don' know that they will recognize me an' Bailey, but I don' know that they won't, either."

"It's all good." Nung watched the terrain whizzing by. "About a quarter mile before we get there, you can let me out. I'll ride on the blind side of the trailer with my rifle, ready for whatever they pull."

"I sure hope this works," Bailey mumbled mostly to herself,

growing nervous that they had settled on using her plan. "What are we going to do if there are women or children at the gas station?"

Caleb made a clicking sound with his tongue. "I hadn't thought of that. We don't really wanna kill these guys, unless they force our hand. So I'd say we leave them be. Hell, I'd love to get my bike back, but if it keeps the peace, they can have it."

Staring at his profile, Bailey considered how unlike his father he was. The older Cross had obviously tried to mold his sons in his own image, but in the end, Caleb had become his own person. *Yes, he would be capable of taking lives if that were necessary.* But at the same time, he had a soft streak that made him irresistible as a human being. *And as a lover.*

Watching the remaining patches of snow flying by in the darkness and shining in the moonlight, the girl smiled at the idea of who had turned out to be her one and only. *He hasn't asked me to marry him yet.* She pondered their situation. *When this is over, I'm going to push the issue.* Just because their world had been broken didn't mean they should give up on what they believed. *Or on our future.*

Stopping as planned, Nung jumped out and circled around behind the trailer. In place, he whacked the metal surface firmly, causing it to ring like a deep kettle drum, signaling Caleb they could move out. Approaching the spot where the road widened, Bailey slid forward in her seat, grasping the headrest before her and peering around it. "Why's it so dark?"

"They have no power," Caleb supplied. "Whatever their backup plan was, if they had one, it's all used up."

Pulling the long rig under the canopy above the pumps, he noted that the front door to the station stood wide open, with the front glass shattered on the ground outside, broken from the inside. "Stay here," he commanded gruffly. Taking his pistol and a flashlight, he exited the vehicle and proceeded to the entrance, calling loudly, "Hello? Anybody here?"

Not getting any response, Caleb chose to skirt the structure, locating a bathroom on the end that appeared undisturbed, with toilet paper still on the roll. On the back side, the wide, thick door appeared forced, with the handle and frame badly damaged. Using his light to illuminate the interior, he kept his weapon pointed everywhere he looked, ready to shoot anything that moved. The back turned out to be a small living quarters, which lay in a shambles.

Working his way through, the place had obviously been cleaned out, with every shelf in the small convenience store bare. Even the racks of cigarettes had been cleared from behind the register. Scowling at the mess, he exited through the front door, waving at Nung, who still watched from behind the trailer. "All clear."

Opening the driver's side, he reached in and killed the engine. "You can get out if you want. I don't think those guys actually belonged here an' maybe had taken over the place like they wanted to do with ours. Either way, there's a toilet on the end, but I have no idea if it actually works. Th' place's been cleaned out, an' I bet Pouty hit them at some point during th' storm as well, or someone else did."

"They made a nice target, out in th' open like this," Amanda pointed out, opening her door to stretch her legs. "We need t' keep an eye out in case someone's still watchin' th' place."

"Agreed." Caleb grinned at Bailey. "You wanna get out or hang out in here. We may have a long wait, since we can't move until Pouty makes theirs."

"We should get some sleep," the girl suggested, "in shifts so that someone is keeping a lookout for the plane to fly over before they head to the town."

"That sounds like a good plan," Nung agreed. "You girls get some rest. We'll wake you in four hours and take a turn ourselves."

Amanda didn't argue, moving to the front seat so Bailey could stretch out in the back, not realizing how tired she was until she closed her eyes. Within minutes, both were sound asleep.

Pete found the keys to the interlopers' Jeep in the ignition, where Caleb had left them. "I wonder why they never told us what happened," he pondered aloud as he cranked the engine. Taking the dirt paths to the gate between the stables and what remained of the arena, he felt fairly certain he knew the answer. *Taking a man's life is a private thing.* Not something the girl would have been proud of or want to share.

Outside the gate, he didn't bother to close it, having Carson following on a four-wheeler to give him a ride back in a few minutes. Arriving at the blacktop, he turned around about two hundred yards from the front gate so that the vehicle faced parallel to the compound. Climbing out, he glared down the road, wondering if the kids had made it over to the gas station yet and how they were faring.

"This far enough away?" Carson queried, pulling up beside him.

"Yeah." Pete clamped him on the shoulder. "Too far and we lose accuracy on the launcher. Let me drive."

Scooting back, the boy let the elder have the front seat, and they closed the fence once they were back inside. Over at the armory, everyone had been assigned a weapon, and John was sketching positions on a map of the front wall.

"Pete," he called when they arrived, "I'm gonna take charge o' the RPG. We only got two shells, so it'll be vital that both shots count."

"Agreed," Peter nodded. "I'm much better with a rifle anyways. Does everyone know their place?"

"Yes, sir." Jennifer grinned while looking at Kristen. "We're ready t' do whatever we gotta do."

"Tha's good." John wafted a hand towards the front wall. "This is gonna get messy. An' I jus' want you t' know we can do this. I mean, if that scrawny little outsider can take down a man, I expect you girls can as well."

"Yes, sir." Kristen giggled, following the group to the front gate. "How long do you think we'll have t' wait?"

"No idea." He grimaced, climbing the ladder. "If they don' come before dawn, it'll be likely we won' see 'em until dark. We'll play it by ear." Glancing up at the light towers they had set up directly in the middle of the gate, he grinned. "If they attack us at night, we'll have a decided advantage with those things. Thank God they didn't steal or destroy 'em when they were here."

"I don't think they paid much attention to what was in the hangar." Peter slapped him on the back. "They were more interested in food an' weapons at the time."

Taking their positions along the narrow band of bricks, the group didn't have long to wait. Off in the distance, a vehicle became visible, followed by another. Watching them coming down the road, John grew tense, aware that they were moving at a high rate of speed. "Silly bastards. Where the fuck's their headlights?"

"Maybe they think they're being sneaky," Peter observed. Seeing them approaching the vehicle that had been intended to divert their course, he swore loudly. "Oh, son of a bitch!"

Never hitting its brakes, the first in the line of what turned out to be five trucks and three SUVs smashed into the parked vehicle, the second plowing in behind it. Watching the chain of events unfold before them, his jaw hung open in disbelief. "Hit the lights!" His voice loud over the sound of the vehicles revving their engines as they left the blacktop, he amended the order. "Fire at will!"

With the bright floodlights glaring down upon them, the group never stood a chance. Using one of his overpowered rockets, the oldest Cross blasted the SUV that seemed to be leading the charge across the field, as if it wanted to reach the north gate. As soon as it exploded, the remainder of the drivers spun their front ends around in retreat.

With expert marksmanship, the girls deflated tires and took down any targets that presented themselves along the way. Realizing that two vehicles were going to get away, John turned to Devon. "We gotta stop 'em. Le's take th' chopper an' get ahead of 'em."

Getting down off the wall in haste, the pair climbed into the helicopter, and John rested a rifle and the launcher between his legs. "I only got one shot, so you'll have t' get on the other driver with this as soon as I get the lead vehicle taken out."

"What abou' damagin' th' road?"

"Fuck th' road," he scowled. "It's already trashed. We have t' stop 'em before they get on th' main highway. Tha's all that matters."

Flying over the top of them only a mile before the cattle guard, both men knew it was going to be close. Setting the machine down, Devon cut the blades, warning his companion, "Watch yurself." Rifle in hand, he climbed out of his side, taking a knee and setting up.

On the other side, John braced himself and sent the rocket flying. The fireball massive, the trailing vehicle slammed on its brakes, skidding as Devon took his shot, shattering the glass and spraying grey matter. His body falling limp, the pressure on the pad released, causing the remaining SUV to slam into the burning wreckage. Only one man attempted to escape the carnage, and the large black hands were steady when he made the kill shot, bringing Pouty's attempt to take Lawson down to an end.

TWENTY-TWO

Enough is Enough

CALEB HEARD the sound of the single-engine plane in the distance. "I think that's our sign." Moving to the edge of the awning, he shaded his eyes against the morning light. "Yup, that's them. Time to go!"

Spinning, he wafted a hand at Nung. "So much for naps!" Opening the driver's door, "'Manda," he gave the girl a shake while the other man roused the one in the back.

"Four hours already?" The blonde frowned, sliding out of the seat.

"No." Caleb hopped into the vacated spot. "We're up. Get in, an' let's roll!"

Flying down the asphalt, the group could see the dark smoke billowing ahead of them. "Oh my God!" Bailey gasped. "That's right up next to the gate!"

Seeing the chopper sitting in their path, the group pulled up and climbed out, while Caleb demanded, "What's going on?"

"We had to alter the plan." John met them in front of the grill, clamping his son on the shoulder. "They brought a mess o' vehicles an' men, an' they had a CB radio, so we can bet Pouty knows things didn' end well for them."

"So what're we gonna do?" Bailey glared at the line of vehicles that stood along the road.

"We're gonna take the fight to them. Enough is enough." Peter nodded at his niece. "An' we aren't taking any more. The helicopter is going to fly ahead and survey the area. We've got six vehicles of our own, an' we're taking all the firepower we can handle. We're gonna attack the front side an' try to sneak in from the plane on the rear to steal the kids back."

"What about getting our animals?" Amanda appeared doubtful.

"We can make it on what we got." John frowned. "Our people are more important. We also wanna send a message loud an' clear. *We* hold the upper hand, an' any survivors should be *terrified* o' even thinkin' about comin' after us again."

Bailey shuddered, reaching for Caleb's hand. "We kill them all?"

"Everyone we see." Peter nodded at her. "If you want to hang back here, we understand. Carson's on the four-wheeler, an' he'll give you a ride back to The Ranch if you would rather go home."

"No way!" Her green eyes flashed. "I'm in this the same as the rest of you." The blond man gave her a squeeze. "Anything we need to know before we get there?"

Moving to the shoulder, Don used a stick to make a rough map. "We're gonna split up. Their streets are open an' not well protected. Plus, Bonny says that the downtown area is all burned. We move around, shooting anyone we see."

The girl wiped at a tear. "How do you know we won't get any of us?"

"We know where they are." Peter added a few boxes to the map. "We're gonna land out here an' move in while you guys have them distracted on the other side of town. Don't worry. We'll get the boys back, and the girls for that matter."

"How long are we going to keep this up?"

The two older men exchanged a glance. "We're gonna set fire to a few more buildings. We made some of those sticky bombs and will use them from a distance. Keep picking them off when they come out. We have an ass ton of ammo from us an' them, so we can keep that up for a while. Caleb, you bring the truck an' trailer around this way once the fires are set. When you reach the farms, the barn is on this end, an' you can load up some of the animals if you're able."

"Ok." He ran a finger through his spikes. "Are these guys still ridin' with me?"

"Amanda an' Bailey are with you, son," John explained. "We need Nung to ride in another vehicle. That gives us one driver an' one shooter in all six of 'em. You guys are the seventh, an' hopefully that'll be enough for us to get the job done."

Glaring at the men, Caleb swallowed visibly, and Bailey knew their plan didn't sit well with him. *Part of that softness that makes him so special,* she sighed. "It's ok, baby," she tried to reassure him. "This's how it has to be if we want to get our family back and make sure we're safe from now on."

"I'm not so sure about that." He shook his head slightly. "But I have to admit, I don't have a better plan. Le's mount up an' get movin'. The longer we wait, the more prepared they'll be."

Arriving at the township a few minutes later, the lead vehicle made a right turn onto a side street, heading for their target. Following the line of cars in their pickup, the girl observed aloud, "If they got any kind of warning, shouldn't they be moving around, getting ready for us?"

"Obviously, they didn' get the word. CB radio's not like a cell phone," Caleb explained. "You gotta have a good signal on both ends or you don' get through."

Bailey nodded. "I guess so." Hearing gunshots ahead of them, she could not tear her eyes away, watching the bodies fall in front of a house. "Oh God!"

"Don't watch, little bit," he warned in a shaky voice. "This is a day we won't ever forget."

Unable to heed his advice, the girl continued to glare as the rest of their group executed their plan without a hitch. Seeing the flames on the sides of several structures, she wiped at her tears. "We go now?"

"Yeah," he agreed, making the turn and following the road that led to the outskirts of the community.

In the distance, Bailey could see a farmhouse, with several people moving around in front of it. "Jess!" she screamed uncontrollably, her flow coming on full blast. "Holy shit! They're alive!" Her cry taking her partner by surprise, he surmised she had actually expected to find that the twins had died or been killed at some point since their disappearance.

The truck stopping next to the barn, Bailey exited and paused to watch the forms moving in the distance, headed towards their small plane that would carry them to safety. "Thank you, Jesus!"

"The're fine, little bit," Caleb interrupted her thoughts. "We need t' move fast an' get what we can."

Amanda took charge of selecting the animals. "We need two roosters and at least six hens." Opening the cages, she claimed them from their pen, skillfully collecting the beasts. "Caleb, you two go get us some hogs. Remember t' get a couple o' males an' the rest females."

Following him, Bailey tried not to let her worry over the others distract her. Entering the barn, she blinked into the dim light. "Which way?"

Hearing the noise around him, the man made his best guess within the massive structure. "Come on." Making his way through the maze of pens, he quickly realized that the greedy bastards had not needed what they had taken from The Ranch. "They had tons o' animals! There's no way all o' this came from what we had," he concluded.

"So which ones do we take?"

Locating a pen full of young males, he opened the gate. "Run a few o' these into the trailer an' drop that divider we put in there t' shut 'em in. Let the rest go, an' let them worry about gettin' their stock back."

Doing as he instructed, the girl managed to get three of the pigs cornered and sealed in, deciding three was better than trying for two and ending up with less.

Returning to him when her task had been completed, she noted that Amanda had joined him as well. "Chickens all set?"

"Yeah." The taller girl nodded. "All caged, ready t' load. I like the looks o' that sow an' her piglets." She extended a long finger to point. "Can you toss down a hay bale in the trailer, an' le's load them next?"

"Sure," Caleb agreed, grabbing a set of hooks off the wall and doing as she instructed.

Running the mother hog out when their bed was ready, the trio gathered the babes, placing them in their new nest and using the next piece of plywood to create the small stall.

"Room for a few more females." Caleb approved of their work.

Making their selection, the cages of fowl went in last, and the massive tailgate closed with a clang. "Nice work, ladies," he praised, waving them towards the cab of their ride.

A few minutes later, they cleared the tiny burrow, and the rest of their comrades fell in line behind them, leaving what was left of Pouty to smolder in the late afternoon sun.

TWENTY-THREE

Can't Stop the Tide

THE ROAD back to The Ranch seemed twice as long as the way over. Bailey glared out the window, watching the sun move towards the west, beating down on them through the window of their transport. Her mind racing, she sighed. "You know, we can't stop the tide. I have a bad feeling this battle will ebb and flow for many months and maybe even years to come."

"Let's hope not," Caleb countered, reaching for her hand. "Le's hope they got the message, an' we can leave each other alone."

Arriving at the cattle guard, he eased his load through the turn, then worked his way around the vehicles that continued to emit a fine wisp of black smoke. "Man, a lot of people died today."

"How many o' ours, do ya think?" Amanda voiced from the back seat, breaking her extended silence.

"Hopefully not any," Bailey replied firmly. "We already lost too many. More than we should have." Her tear spilled over at the thought of Connie, Martha, and the others. "We should all still be here and would be if it hadn't been for them wanting what we had."

"You can't really blame them," Caleb countered, causing both females to glare at him, so he clarified. "We coulda been a threat.

We knew a great deal about them, but they didn't really know anything about us. I don't think they wanted our stuff as much as they wanted..." He searched for the right words. "They didn't wanna worry about us coming up short an' goin' after them."

"That's not true," Bailey accused. "They had Don, Luis, and Devon pretending to join them and feeding them information. They weren't afraid of us."

"False information," Amanda clarified. "Jus' wanna keep the record straight." She adjusted herself in her seat uncomfortably.

"Well, false, but they didn't know that," Bailey continued. "For all they knew, they had the truth and should have known we weren't going to be aggressive. All we wanted was to be left alone."

Caleb flicked his eyes to meet Amanda's in the rear-view mirror. The girl did not smile while she glared at him, aware that his new woman was very naive. Eventually breaking the connection, she turned her attention to the gate they had arrived at, heaving a sigh of relief when they pulled up outside the barn to unload their haul.

Once the animals had all been returned to their pens, the group made their way down into Lawson, where a good meal awaited them. Entering the great hall, Bailey's eyes scanned the tables, chairs, and heads, looking for the two that mattered the most.

Spying the identical brown tops, she shrieked, "Boys!" Dodging around the pit, she reached them, grabbing them both the best she could. Her cry a loud wail. "You guys are ok!"

"Yes," they answered in unison, clinging to the girl and blubbering loudly. "It was so horrible!" Jess elaborated.

"I'm sure it was," his sister sobbed. "I was so scared I was going to lose you!" Holding them for several minutes, they wept openly, while the remainder of the community left them alone, watching from their chairs as they dined.

Soon, the trio released one another and took their seats. Caleb had fixed a plate for the girl and grinned broadly when she sat down to devour her first food since their planning session the night before.

"Is everyone here?" she asked nervously, ready to survey the group and hear about their losses.

"Everyone who went over has returned," Peter supplied. "With our last group that is. We lost four, as we can only assume that Chris and Martha are in fact gone." He cut Caleb a doleful glance. "I'm really sorry about that."

"I know," the younger male placed his elbows on the table, leaning on clenched fists under his chin. "She will be missed by everyone, I think."

Running her fingers firmly down his back, Bailey could feel the tension in his muscles. "Yes, she will," she agreed in a quiet voice. "But we gained one." She indicated the young woman who sat alone at the moment. "I assume she's one of us now."

Pete watched the girl thoughtfully. "Yeah, I reckon she is."

Exhausted, the group made their way to bed early that night, only briefly discussing if they should set a guard. "I doubt they would be stupid enough to attack us, especially this soon," Peter reassured everyone. "Maybe in a day or a week or some time down the line, they will get bold enough to try, but for right now, they are deeply wounded. It'll be a while before they do anything, I'm pretty certain."

As if in agreement, Caleb slipped his hand into hers, leading Bailey to the tiny room that they shared, before he realized their household had grown.

Putting a sheet on the couch, she made it into a makeshift bed for one of the boys, pointing out, "I guess we'll have to rearrange the sleeping quarters again."

"Not tonight." Peter coughed. "We're all beat. Everyone get down an' get quiet." Within fifteen minutes, the only sound in the entire structure was that of snores while the small, close-knit community slept.

TWENTY-FOUR

To the Victor

THE FOLLOWING morning came late in Lawson. The sun had been up for hours when Amanda led her crew, under armed escort, to the surface inside the barn. To everyone's relief, the animals were safe and eager to be fed, a dog and her wriggly pups included.

Leaving the girls to their duty, Don and Devon scaled the wall to survey the area in front of their compound. The seven vehicles that stood in the pasture and dotted the blacktop served as a dim reminder of how close they had come to losing everything they had worked for.

The women had gathered the bodies the previous afternoon while the attacking group had made their move against Pouty. A hole had been dug not far from the wreckage; there they had been placed and covered unceremoniously. What once had been the leaders of a small community now lay in an unmarked grave that would remain so, their very existence to be forgotten in time.

"To the victors go the spoils." Don laughed, shaking his head while he glanced across the streets and structures beneath them. "O' course, we only have a few more rides comin' at most before we're out o' fuel."

"Yeah," Devon agreed, "but we made it. An' I got my wife an' baby girl. An' yurs'll be here soon enough!"

"Yeah, I guess I'll marry that girl. She seems all right." He laughed loudly. "Caleb's the one I think got the short end o' the stick. That little red-headed bitch...not sure how long she's gonna hold out here."

Devon's deep round rumble joined with his. "I think dat li'l girl jus' might surprise you!" Climbing down, he moved to return to his wife to help out if he could.

Back inside for a late lunch, a meeting was called, and the chairs were assembled around the pit. On the cushions below sat the new *menfolk*, which included Caleb, Don, Devon, and Nung.

Standing in the center of the gathering, John coughed loudly, ready to bring the proceedings to order. "Well, we made it," he huffed, broken hearted at the loss of his spouse. "You all know I wasn't the best husband," he admitted, his words laden with sorrow, "but she was a damned fine wife. I didn' appreciate her near enough or tell her as much as I shoulda..." His voice trailed away, and he cleared his throat loudly.

"So things are changed," he continued, wringing his hands. "We gots t' go on, here. We gots new families formin'." He cut his eyes over at his son. "An' we got a bright future despite the turmoil that has overtaken the world at large."

Seeing a few of the women fidget, he grinned wryly. "I know you all wonder what's happened out there. We all do. An' maybe someday we'll find out who has survived an' where they are. But we made this place so's we could do without 'em, an' I think after what happened with Pouty, stayin' away from the rest o' humanity, at least for the time bein', is a smart move."

"Amen," a female voice agreed.

"With that bein' said," he continued, "we also need t' get more into a normal routine. Get outta this hole for one thing. An' get back to the houses an' the surface. Clean all this up an' keep it ready in case we ever need t' take refuge down here in th' future. If our winters have been changed for th' permanent, this may be where we wait 'em out, schoolin' the young an' keepin' our energy usage down."

Several of the community members were nodding their agreement while Bailey surveyed the lot, her mind turning. "What about the houses?" she spoke up, unafraid of interrupting him. "Will we be able to construct any new ones?"

"Naw, little bit." He turned so he could see her. "But don' you worry. We'll be rearranging the households so that all o' the buildin's are put to good use." He grinned when he spoke, giving the girl a fit of crawling agitation in her gut. "Anyone else got a question?"

When no one else spoke up, he began his conclusion. "We'll hold a little conference this afternoon. Decide who's gonna be occupying what now an' lay out those plans. Then we'll begin our return to the surface tomorrow." Leaving it at that, he climbed out of the circle and made his way to his quarters, where he could be alone for a bit before they faced the task of dividing up what had once belonged to him and his wife and the life it had taken them over twenty years to build.

Caleb rose from his seat slowly, his eyes meeting Bailey's squarely. His palms sweaty, he had only been half listening while his father spoke. Climbing out of the pit, he moved to stand before the tall, auburn-haired beauty, arriving face to face and stopping only inches from her. Exhaling loudly, a slow grin covered his features. "Are you ready?"

"Ready for what?" She smiled up at him, the worms in her guts growing wings, taking flight inside her belly.

"To be my wife." He reached for her hand. "I wish I had a ring to offer you, but I'm afraid th' jewelry store never made it t' completion."

The girl giggled at his silliness. "Oh, so I don't get a ring?"

"I guess not." He shook his head slightly. "Do I need a ring, or can we get by without it?"

She nodded slowly, stepping towards him, her arms finding

their way around his neck. "I love you, Caleb Cross. And I will always be yours, ring or no ring, so long as I live."

"So long as we both shall live," he corrected, his hands on her hips, giving them a squeeze.

"You see it your way, and I'll see it mine." She pressed her lips to his, happy that he had finally taken the plunge.

TWENTY-FIVE

Sunshine and Daisies

"COME ON, BAILEY," the tall blonde's voice whined slightly. "We don' have all day."

"I know." The shorter girl grinned. "I just want a few more." She clipped the long stems. "There, that'll be enough." Getting to her feet, she followed her best friend across the field, her mind tracing the time that she had known the young woman and what all they had endured before Amanda had earned that distinction.

Arriving at the house, they began cleaning, going over the entire duplex. Putting the flowers in a large vase in the center of the table, she grinned at the arrangement. "Do you think Jen will like them?"

"She's gonna love them," Amanda tossed at her while freshening the cushions on the couch and folding the short stack of blankets next to the crib. "It was pretty lucky she had a boy, although that means sharin' clothes with her'll be tougher since Hope's a girl." She cut her eyes over warily. "Whadda ya suppose you're gonna have?"

Bailey's green eye's shot up to look at her companion, a daisy resting between her fingers. "Uh, what do you mean?" she replied coyly.

"Oh, come on, Bail," the older girl moaned. "You've been showin' signs fur weeks, even before yur weddin'. I thought by now you woulda made the announcement."

Her cheeks flaming, she dropped the delicate petals. "I didn't think anyone knew!"

Laughing loudly, her friend moved to give her a hug. "Everyone knows, Bailey-girl. You've waited almost four months, an' your belly's gonna pop out any time now. It's all right though. We're all happy for you!" Leading her to the exit, they crossed the street with the warm south Texas sun shining down on their scalps.

Climbing the steps to her own duplex, Bailey sighed loudly. "Ok, yes, Caleb and I are expecting. Probably about the time the worst part of winter is on us again." She shook her head ruefully.

"It's all good." Amanda indicated the far side of the compound through the wall, where her mother now ran the ranch house. "Mom's been enjoyin' her role as designated nanny, so I'm sure she won' mind addin' your little one t' the brood."

"Yes, but Jen's will still be a baby, too. Besides, I think Kathy was a bit upset we didn't wait." They left the structure, ready to go and see the other girl home with her new infant. Pausing to give Blackie fresh water, she patted her pup firmly on the ribs. "Man, he's getting big," she commented to herself before continuing the discussion. "But she estimates the due date as Christmas, so I think that's a good omen."

"That's cool. Hope'll be nearly a year old by then," the blonde replied as they strolled down the road. "How're things over in the greenhouse, anyways? Will we be ready fur winter?"

"Oh, yes." Bailey grinned. "Running smooth and putting out a bumper crop. I assume everything is good in the barn?" Her mind briefly flashed to the hog they had butchered her first summer there. "I'm really glad you got that part. I don't think I could stomach all that blood and guts."

"It's not s' bad. The new division o' labor is workin' well, an' we're back up t' speed on the animal populations. We'll be butcherin' a few in the fall, an' things'll be back t' normal. Even if we get snowed on again like last year, we got it covered." Amanda reached for the door to enter the med center. "Anyone home?" she called loudly.

"Not yet," Jennifer replied with a giggle. "Are you here t' get me there?"

"Sure are." She helped gather her things. "Bailey, you ready t' go get the cart?"

"Yes, I can do that." She left the two young women and jogged down the dirt path alone. Arriving at the small garage where the golf cart was stored behind the Cross house, she discovered her husband out back, messing with the tools in the shed. Pausing, she called out playfully, "And what are you up to, Mr. Cross?"

"Gonna get on repairin' those two turbines we lost last winter…if I can." He grinned. "Still tryin' t' figure it out. I think I got it this time, though. You girls gettin' Jennifer situated?"

"About to." Bailey switched on the small cart, adjusting herself into the seat. "Thank you for getting this thing running. It's come in very handy these last few months, and I was afraid it was broken down for good."

"Yes, ma'am." He tipped an imaginary hat to her. "It's rechargeable, an' that's the best part. Had to get it runnin' for sure."

"I guess so." She patted the seat next to her. "Want to ride with us?"

"I thought you'd never ask." He swung under the canopy and plopped down onto the cushion. "But I can't stay long. I really need t' get as much done as I can before the weather changes."

"We all do," Bailey agreed. "Are we having fireworks again this year? You know tomorrow's the Fourth of July."

"I dunno." He held on to the support pole while she swung their ride around. "After all tha's happened, I'm not sure what everyone will think o' that."

"All the more reason to do it, baby." The girl grinned, a warm feeling overtaking her. "It's our freedom and our survival that we're celebrating, after all."

Pulling up in front of the med center, he slid over behind the wheel when she vacated the spot. "I'll wait for you here."

The two girls inside had been watching for her and came out as soon as they pulled up. Taking the two seats in the back, the pair chattered about baby talk, while Bailey rode in the front, feeling a little left out at the moment. *But it'll be my turn soon enough.* She smiled to herself, her hand running across her belly and the small pooch that had begun to form.

Climbing the steps to her porch, Jen gripped the railing, then made her way inside. "Wow!" she exclaimed. "Sunshine an' daisies, a perfect homecomin' for my new angel!"

Bailey beamed, glad her surprise had been noticed. Sliding his arms around his wife's waist, Caleb whispered in her ear, "I'll see what I can do about the celebration. After all, you're right. We've come a long way, an' I'm so glad t' have you by my side, Mrs. Cross."

She smiled at her married name, still not fully accustomed to it. "You better get back to work"—she twisted in his arms, planting a firm kiss on his lips—"before you end up at home in the middle of the day."

He laughed loudly. "Boy, you sure turned out t' be a horn dog," he mocked her.

"Only for you." She snickered with another quick kiss before she pushed him away. "I'll see you tonight." Turning to the girls, she announced, "Well, now that my secret is out, I feel like celebrating. Who's with me?"

"Not me." Jen puttered around her kitchen at the moment. "But thank you for puttin' things in order. I'm gonna get me a nap while Jacob's asleep."

"Tha's a great idea." Her sister waggled a finger at her. "You're gonna need it. Babies 're hard work." Turning to Bailey, she looped an arm with hers. "Whatcha got in mind, little bit?"

"Let's go over to the diner, see if they need a hand with dinner or whatever's on the agenda for today."

"Tha's not celebrating!" Amanda laughed loudly. "Get a nap,

sis. We'll see you later," she called, ushering her auburn-haired companion outside. "You sure have settled in here," she complimented as they strolled to the larger structure. "I have t' admit, I didn' think you'd make it."

"Yes," Bailey sighed. "But come to find out this is the perfect place for me. I used to wonder why anyone would choose to live this way. Now…" She shrugged, grinning at the tall blonde. "Now, I can't imagine ever going back to the way things were, even if we could."

"Amen." Amanda nodded, opening the door so they could join the rest of the women of the small community.

"Amen," Bailey echoed under her breath, smiling at the group who were working to provide their collective with the things that mattered most. *And more than just a hot meal or survival.* The girl knew Lawson was about far more than that. *This is about people—family and friends… It's about real life and all the wonderful things one might find in a desert in the middle of nowhere.*

RENDERED
RETAINED
RECOMBINED
COMPLETE BOXED SET

Flowchart

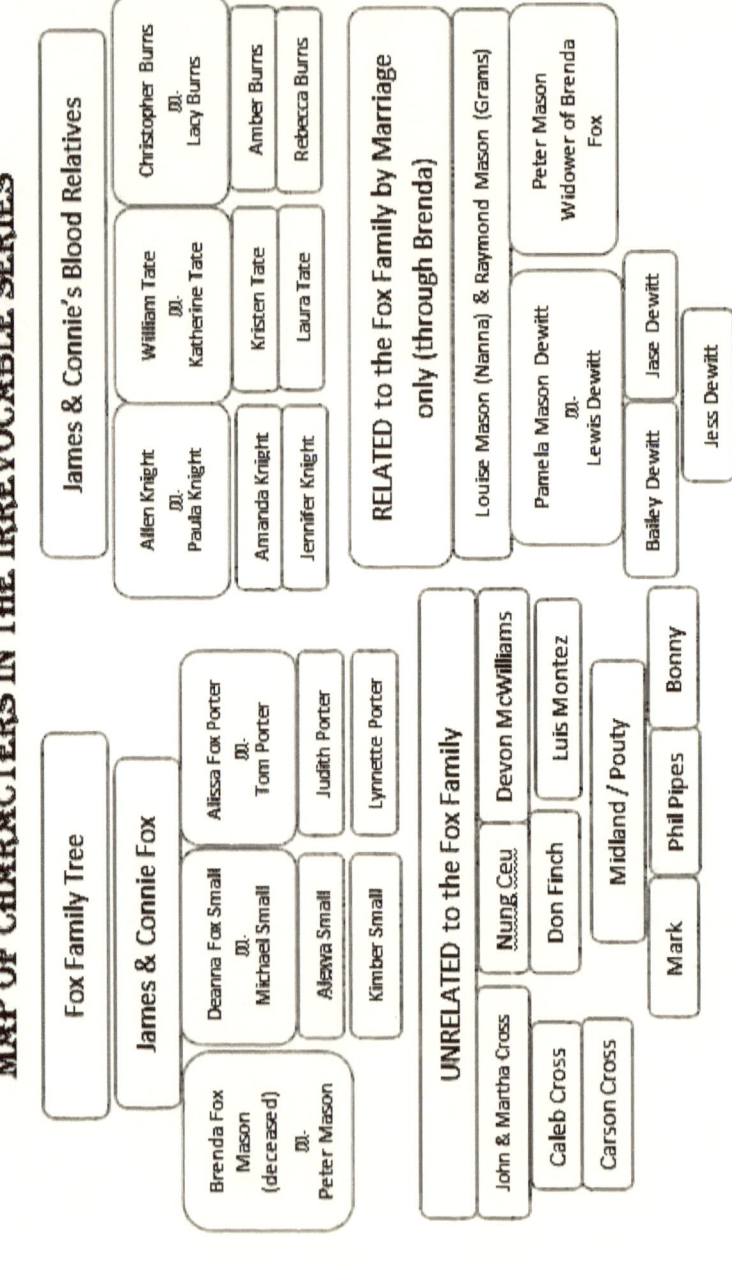

MAP OF CHARACTERS IN THE IRREVOCABLE SERIES

Maps

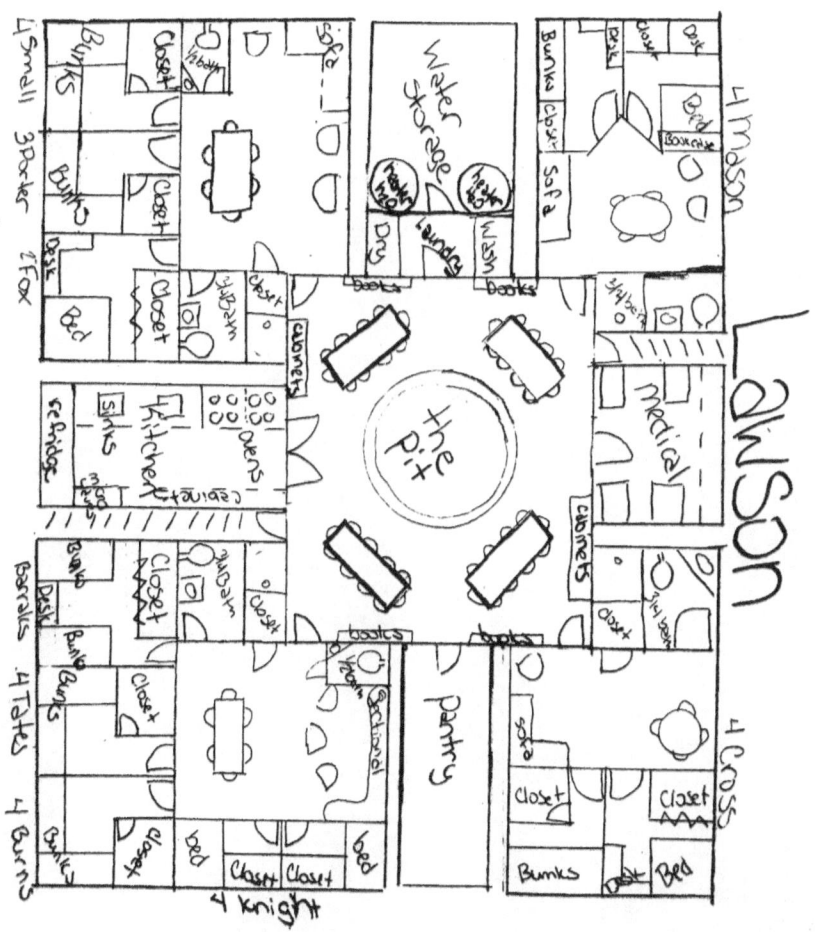

About the Author

Anyone who knows me could tell you, I am a friendly kind of person, never met a stranger and take up conversations anywhere at any time. I work hard, and my mind never seems to shut down, as I wake up often in the middle of the night with ideas pouring out and demanding to be dealt with. Of course that means much of my books were written in the middle of the night.

I grew up and still live in the great state of Texas where everything is bigger, where we have warm weather and a central location. I love my state, my town, and my family, which includes my four sons, my significant other, and many friends as well.

I have thoroughly enjoyed writing this story and hope that you will love reading it just as much. And of course, there will be many more adventures to come.

You can follow Samantha Jacobey at:
Website: www.SamJacobey.com
Facebook: https://www.facebook.com/SamJacobey
Twitter: https://twitter.com/SamJacobey
Pinterest: http://www.pinterest.com/samanthajacobey/

Also by SAMANTHA JACOBEY

http://www.amazon.com/-/e/B00GEB5LX0

A New Life Series – an epic adventure, TORI FARRELL's life IS one wild story... escaped from a biker gang and running from drug lords... used by the FBI and hoping to protect her present from her past... IT'S DARK - IT'S BRUTAL, and it's WORTH EVERY MINUTE OF IT!! (Mature read, 18+ for graphic sexual content and violence, including rape)

Summer Spirit Novella Series - no one EVER had a summer romance like this... Charlie visits another plane, parallel to our own, where Summer Angels and Dark Angels battle over the fate of man. A unique twist on an old idea that will keep you guessing; will Charlie and Clarisse ever find their HEA? (New adult)

Teach Me to Prey – in this standalone thriller, JASON TRUITT and his friends have gotten their way for years. Deceit, sex, and foul play aren't normally covered in the curriculum, but they're doing whatever it takes to get under BECKY STEWART's skin. When one of the boys turns up dead, it's a race against time to save the others; a STUNNING STORY that will get your heart racing and leave you breathless by the end... (New Adult)

The Binding (Unexpected Magic #1) - One cursed diary will change two strangers forever...Can Meri and Rider use her mother's old book to figure out why someone is after them? Or will the guilty party succeed, ripping the tome away before killing them and then slithering back into the darkness... (New Adult)

The Wicked Awakened (Unexpected Magic #2) – a

Halloween novel; a five-hundred-year-old witch wants to turn SARAH MATTHEWS' body into her new home… A twisted tale involving a coven hell bent on seeing that she succeeds. Who will come out on top in this epic battle of wills? (Mature read, 18+ for graphic sexual content and violence)

Sweet Christmas Series - Life isn't always sweet, even for girls called Candy. Candice Parker's life has never been easy. Plagued by losses and setbacks, each day is a struggle for the petite brunette and her young son. When fireman Gary enters her world, he is one mistake she refuses to make; but after tragedy strikes, she may not have a choice. (New Adult)

The Dragon of Eriden Series - Amicia Spicer led a simple life, until she discovered it had all been a lie… On her deathbed, Arely Spicer confessed to her only daughter that she had been found by, not born to her mother and father. Sad news to be certain, the idea of having a family of flesh and blood waiting to be reunited sent the young, independent woman on the adventure of a lifetime. Little did she know, a dragon's heart beat within her chest and her journey would be more perilous than she could have imagined... (New Adult)

Also from the Lavish family

Behind Blue Eyes
Sara J. Bernhardt
http://mybook.to/BehindBlueEyesSeries

A father's desire to save his child presents him with an unthinkable choice that leaves him darker than human, forced to roam through time alone as he searches for the place he belongs.

Adam Gold – Book 1: Fleeing the French invasion of Geneva Switzerland in the 1700s, Adam Gold books passage to America with his family. On the ship, Adam's daughter falls fatally ill. A mysterious man comes to Adam with a way to save his child by turning Adam into something darker than human.

The Medallion – Book 2: Adam Gold, an immortal with sweet eyes of blue, rushes through the centuries on a quest for reason and a thirst for revenge. To cope with his pain and regret, he sleeps away the years and awakes in a new era with a powerful, ancient vampire who sets her sights on him.

Golden Shackles – Book 3: When the ancient queen, Sekhmet snatches up Adam, he is faced with a terrifying decision. To help aid her in her vile plans or dare to stand against her.

Plus 3 more segments!

Rosinanti Series
Kevin J. Kessler
http://myBook.to/RosinantiSeries

The Rosinanti Dragons are no more. Since their extinction nearly one thousand years ago these primal powerhouses have fallen into the obscurity of history's forgotten lore. In that time, humans have come to dominate the world of Terra, peacefully ignorant to one horrifying truth: ancient evil stirs around them, waiting to reclaim its lost world.

For Valentean Burai, animus warrior of the kingdom of Kackritta, the details surrounding humanity's victory over the Rosinanti are more than just a history lesson. The long-buried mysteries of this archaic conflict may hold the answers that he has so desperately sought regarding his own past.

As the awful truth of the Rosinanti's supposed demise comes to light, Valentean must stand together with Seraphina, a magically gifted princess, to embark upon a mission to maintain order and light throughout Terra. Only together can these two lifelong friends face down the resurgence of the Rosinanti legacy and combat the greatest threat their world has ever known.

www.ingramcontent.com/pod-product-compliance
Lightning Source LLC
Chambersburg PA
CBHW020409150626
46554CB00012B/424